FORE!

Introduction

"Success depends almost entirely on how effectively you learn to manage the game's two ultimate adversaries: the course and yourself."

- Jack Nicklaus

"It is forbidden to Kill; therefore, all murderers are punished unless they kill in large numbers and to the sound of trumpets".

- Voltaire

"Golf is the closest game to the game we call life. You get the bad breaks from good shots; you get good breaks from bad shots – but you have to play it where it lies".

- Bobby Jones

Golf is a game where the ball always lies poorly and the player always lies well. Luckily, violence on a golf course is rare, at least amongst golfers. I have seen plenty of clubs come under attack, clubs mercilessly consigned to sink in ponds, lakes and even in the sea. Bushes and trees attacked. Clubs snapped, bent out of shape, decapitated. I have seen a squirrel and a rabbit both succumb to their untimely ends thanks to a little flying white ball. Maybe they didn't understand the meaning of the term FORE! So pay attention when you hear that call. And if you are ever caught on a golf course during a storm and are afraid of lightning do as Lee Trevino says and hold up a 1-iron. Not even God can hit a 1-iron.

I grew up playing golf, thanks to my father JJ and I have grown to enjoy the challenge of playing against the course and playing match play against an opponent, a different type of challenge (JJ was a fierce competitor) and most importantly of all the challenge of overcoming the demons in the mind. Swing that club with as few thoughts interfering with your goal as possible. See ball, hit ball. Here is to you JJ. Always in my thoughts. I hope the courses in the Sky really are as perfect as I hear they are. I will join you for a game when my time comes but I hope that our tee time isn't any time too soon. I still have a few courses to play down here, divots to leave, putts to miss, shots to forget and maybe to remember. FORE!

With thanks to Lola, Isobel, Erin, Patrick, Bethany…always my inspiration.

And thanks also to Rob Jones, my unexpected but eager test audience who kept asking for more Chapters.

Contents

Chapter 1

Sandy Lie and the 19th hole

"Golf is a lot of walking, broken up by disappointment and bad arithmetic."

"FORE" the call came over the radio. Detective Chief Superintendent Eagle has asked for some info on the incident. "Golf club… four golfers dead. Get it FORE." Eagle didn't get it. He was grumpy after a restless night's sleep and was now on his way to visit a bunch of stuffed up twats dressed like Rupert the bear. "FORE …you know it's the warning in golf."

"Just let me know what has actually happened." As he turned the car into a corner several minutes away from his destination, a little too fast, a splash of coffee spilled out over the cup lid he hadn't quite closed well enough. He blamed a design flaw with the travel mug. They call it golf because the other four-letter words were taken. Eagle had heard this line before, but his four-letter word of choice was FUCK. The way he expelled it the four-letter word became more like a 16-letter repetition. 4 bodies. Forensics already on the scene. What a start to a Sunday morning.

“Can you let me know what you heard outside the victim’s room last night … I am told that you might have heard something important which might help us”… Eagle did his best to sound interested despite a pounding headache.

“Well, there was banging, you know real crashing around like”… Frank Conroy was a red-faced jovial man in his mid-fifties. His eyes danced as he spoke. This is not our homicidal golfer Eagle already knew that. Eagle had a knack for knowing who he could trust in life, who could be believed and who was quite frankly talking bullshit. Frank continued…. "Well now Seamus was steaming drunk so had already gone to bed so like I when I came up, I was trying not to wake him or make any noise coz sure then he would be pishing all night, very weak bladder that man …(pause) And so, when I got near the room then I heard the commotion … (another pause) I stopped just outside to find the key card but then next door I heard someone shout”….

Frank raises his voice accordingly for this bit…

“I am going to feckin ram this club so far up your HOLE (emphasis on hole - Frank likes to tell a story) your bollocks will pop out of your eyeballs.”

Frank lets this hang in the air dramatically and the use of the word hole was noted down in Eagle's notebook for reasons he would revert to at a later date, then Frank interrupted his own pause gesticulating with his hands and particularly his thumbs as though he were holding an imaginary joystick before adding "and then it went quiet."

"Aha" Eagle murmured as he took notes trying to suppress any possible laughter at what was a highly entertaining delivery. He was accompanied by PC Irons who had shown him to the three dead bodies on the ground floor, well ground level, before leading him to victim number four primarily to catch up with the pathologist, Professor Nick Green. Two of the dead party, had been roomies, room 13. Unlucky for some.

The other poor sod had been found face down in a macabre display in the picturesque green side bunker that engulfed the back of the 18th green beneath the clubhouse balcony like a huge baseball glove. This would usually have been bathed in sunlight for those attending breakfast and wanting to enjoy the view out towards the signature hole at Chorus Hills Country Club. A long par five from an elevated tee box with a green protected by a river on one side and huge moat of sand on the other. The drawbridge over the river to the green might have been a touch excessive but somehow fitted in amongst its illustrious surroundings.

Somehow the view from the breakfast room on this particular morning was less serene, no less spectacular mind you. After all it's not every day that you see a dead body with its bare bottom on display in the sand and flag waving in the wind seemingly pointing to an alternative 19th hole. Not quite the signature view that the Chorus Hills Country Club had adorned across its website and brochures. But a spectacular real-life Banksy, that is if Banksy were a homicidal maniac with a hatred for golf.

PC Irons had found it much harder not to release a snigger which he tried to turn somewhat unsuccessfully into a cough at the mention of the word hole! as accentuated by Frank Conroy or more to the way it was delivered. So, this was the fourth victim, perhaps not in that particular order, not a very happy foursome or four ball. If he was more in tune with his inner golf wanker, or knew anything about the game of Whackfuck (his own personal name for it) he might have made the connection himself but Detective Chief Superintendent Eagle detested golf. The term fourball didn't mean much to him. In fact, as he had driven into the car park after what he considered to be a ridiculously long journey down a meandering driveway protected by row after row of sturdy Oaks, each standing to attention forming a guard of honour, he finally arrived at his destination some four minutes after the Sat Nav had declared he had reached his destination. This had annoyed him immensely. But then again, he was not a patient man.

Eagle suddenly felt decidedly out of place and uncomfortable. 'Golf wankers' he thought as he saw two men dressed in bright red trousers and pastel coloured polo shirts and tank tops unloading equipment out of a spanking new sheer black Land Rover. Look at those Cockwombles he spoke out loud despite being all alone in his own vehicle. It had certainly been an interesting start to the day. Still, he resigned himself to the fact that he might possibly be able to ruin their day by declaring the course closed. Unless they intended to play around the dead body and forensics team.

Despite the rather vocal threat as reported by Frank Conroy, luckily the deceased man in room 127 was not found with any sort of club inserted into his backside. This was a relief not just to the maid who had been asked to open the door, but to all those who had ventured in thereafter. Quite why so many people had been allowed at the scene of the crime was beyond Eagle. The deceased had been hit over the head with something, possibly a golf club (later revealed to be an 8-iron belonging to one of the deceased). He had probably in fact died from a combination of his head injury and his airways being blocked by a golf ball which was lodged deep in the back of his throat. "A good one too. A Titleist Pro V1 …Expensive. Don't want to lose those ones…brand new unused this one …damn shame to put this in the evidence box. Could have taken this one, obviously needs a clean" the pathologist, Professor Nick Green chuckled to himself.

The professor was evidently a golfer. Eagle had of course known this from the moment he had first set eyes on the new pathologist when he was first assigned to the area a couple of years ago. Green had joined him straight from the course in a beautiful green Aston Martin dressed like a court jester to confirm a bad batch of heroine. Multiple drug overdoses via a bad batch in an affluent village should have been straight forward but was over complicated by one of the victims being the daughter of a prominent local MP. A tough case but the two had stood firm despite considerable interference and finger pointing, primarily at police failings to prevent so-called County Lines drugs infiltrating such a peaceful and serene part of the country. Two years had passed in the blink of an eye since then and Green and Eagle were by no means friends, but Eagle counted him as a solid work acquaintance.

Amenable, always pristine even when up to his elbows in blood and guts, Professor Green barely spoke about anything other than golf, well golf and cause of death. Actually, he loved cars too and red wine. Professor Green gave Eagle a very simple lowdown. "So, four victims. Each with significant blunt force trauma to the head. Three golf balls lodged down three throats and one in the anus…. What a bummer." Tough lie. Hard to overlook the one in the bum.

Eagle had already made a note to find out all he could do about the body in the bunker. 'Sandy lie' as the guys from the station were already calling him. Apparently, this was a reference to some old fart who won something once and hit a good shot out of the sand while coincidentally being called Sandy. It was of little interest to Eagle. There was a special kind of anger and humiliation lined up for Sandy Lie. He was left on display and brutalised in a manner that suggested the perpetrator really did not like him. The positioning of that flag was enough to make anyone wince.

"To surmise. Easiest fucking case ever" Nick Green was quick to declare winking at Eagle as he did so. Not a man to be easily phased especially by a bit of claret Nick Green was keen to offer a very simple means of finding the killer. It was a small point of order but something that always sent Eagle's nerves on edge was the manner in which Green was able to unburden himself of his work clothes and stench of death and immediately grab something to eat. Never once acknowledging that he had been dealing with something that would make most stomachs churn he always seemed to be snacking. So now stripped of his scrubs he was simultaneously drinking coffee and munching on an apple. The apple he had grabbed from his car and the coffee provided by the clubhouse. The staff were going about their business in difficult circumstances. A murder would have been a first for the country club. Four seemed excessive.

So the gem from Professor Green. The evidence to concentrate on and don't forget this observation was thus … "There are two sleeves of brand new Pro V1 Titleist golf balls …one with two balls still in place most probably…. And one empty. Quite often the empty sleeve will still be in the golf bag. No one empties the Pro V reserve lightly but also if he only needed one from let's call it sleeve two, for the one up the anus, the other two will still be nestled safely in the comfort of their natural home. That's how it works. You have a maniac who likes golf and who knew the victims who were all struck by what is likely to be a golf club, not necessarily the same club. Three of the victims had a golf ball positioned down their throat. One had one inserted up his rectum and flagpole for good measure. Find the golf balls from the same batch find the killer. The other thing that might give the game away is blood splatter. These guys were hit pretty hard and at least one of them put up a bit of a fight so any signs of injury scratch marks bruising needs to be looked at. Last night's clothes might tell us all we need to know."

Eagle and Green were joined by for want of a better description Eagle's partner in solving crime … Jenny O'Par, a super smart diminutive bundle of energy from County Galway in Ireland who had been listening in as she ghosted in alongside her cranky superior officer. 30 going on 12. She was opinionated and she was honest, brutally honest. Jet black hair and green eyes. Just about the only detective in the Station who could hold their own against Eagle. Not just hold her own but chew him up and spit him out.

"Well, the footprints in the bunker might be telling … given that the dead half naked guy didn't walk in there himself".

"Quite right" Green added "who trapses through the bunker and doesn't rake over the mess they made? … Damn rude." Green had been careful to make sure they had disturbed as little as possible in attending to Sandy Lie. The two gave a fist bump designed solely to agitate Eagle. He shook his head in disapproval.

Wow! Eagle was perturbed. More so by the amount of weight Green was placing on the value of a particular brand of ball than the fact that someone had killed four of his fellow golfers and saw fit to shove a golf ball up one of his fellow 'Whackstick wankers' bottoms. That suggested a special kind of anger. First things first, bag up the evidence so far, take statements, and find out all you can about this fourball and the rest of the chaps in this outfit.

"phones" 'O' Par added… "let's see what these guys have been messaging each other … or if any unusual late-night calls were made".

“That’s if we can find phones. So far only one of four phones belonging to the deceased have been retrieved.” The Professor added almost to himself.

And then it hit him. Eagle understood - yes four balls for a fourball. Four members of the same whackfuck group who all potted off at the same time. This little bit of info had been established but needed to be verified. Potted, whacked…apparently teed off in the same group the day before. Each of them smacked round the head with a golf club and found with a ball down or up an orifice. Whatever connected those four with the killer must have been pretty heavy, given the carnage that has followed because this was not simply a case of wrong place wrong time or indeed some other crime gone wrong. At least it didn’t feel that way to Eagle.

“You know, Green piped up “sex and golf are two of a very small number of activities you can still enjoy even if you are no good at them.”

“That’s great news for you then” O’ Par laughed.

And with that he was off. Pristine as ever. Waltzing off the premises. There was work to do back at the lab, but it had already been a busy morning. He had done all he had wanted to here and his team would finish up and collect the bodies. “Bye Jenny… Eagle” he nodded as he departed, while muttering "Damn shame about those Pro V1s." The nod turned into a shake of the head.

What a start to the annual Birchgrove Irish Golf Society Captains away day. Day one saw 20 golfers tee off. Only 16 made breakfast on day two. Look it was far far worse than that only 16 were alive. Four of the daft buggers had been murdered in the night. £169 might have sounded a good deal at the time for two rounds of golf B&B plus three course dinner. I mean sure you got to play the East and West courses, designed by Ian Woosnam nonetheless, but if you don't even make it through the night, that doesn't seem like such a good offer.

The remaining gaggle of 16 golfers had been gathered in a function room. It was a sombre gathering as you might expect. They were all going to have to be swabbed and agree to have their golf bags, clubs, sticks, whackers, whatever they wanted to call them handed over to be processed. Eagle briefed his team. Each member of the Society would all need to give statements. Eagle was wondering if they had a leader who might make this whole process less onerous. He began to look for some semblance of calm amongst the sea of colour before him. Christ, he thought to himself I hope someone other than the killer amongst this group has some idea of what the hell might have led to the demise of four of the group.

Professor Nick Green had once told him that the worst day of golf beats the best day in the office. That may be true if you spend your days cutting open dead bodies Eagle thought to himself. Give me a day in the office drinking tea and scratching my arse mulling over paperwork over walking around in the wet looking for a little white ball especially if the day ends with your death and a butt-naked open burial with a flag protruding from your butt. Eagle corrected himself Arsehole. Clearly watching too many American dramas.

He was carefully observing those assembled. Naturally, it was a pretty deflated group - split into several smaller groups around the room. Was this a sign of a cluster of alliances or simply a group of guys comforting each other after some pretty horrific news. There was tea, coffee and bacon rolls mostly untouched on the tables. Discounting his officers, he made 15 so that meant someone was missing. Who the fuck was missing and why … momentarily Eagle wondered whether a fifth victim was going to emerge. He called over a PC he vaguely recognised from the station, a newbie, recently transferred, and was about to brief her when there was an almighty rant from the corridor and then from the abyss the walking talking depiction of gout marched in thunderously, red faced and broom up his arse (that's arse not butt). If you are going to barge yourself into a restricted police investigation do so with an air of confidence.

“Fucking outrageous… A qualifier for the club Championship and some fucking dimwit has seen fit to close the course. What the devil is the meaning of this” the voice matched the tosser who emerged to claim it as far as Eagle was concerned.

Since he happened to be closest to the door he intervened and blocked his path introducing himself “I am sorry who are you and what do you want”, in his head he briefly envisaged a scenario where he immediately punched this man out cold. Instead, he used the significant frame (a half decent front row back in the day) to block access.

“Rupert Bogey … club captain and I need to get this course open.”

“Well Mr Bogey that’s not going to happen I am afraid… it’s a crime scene and there is still a dead body in the sandpit on the last hole.”

“You mean the bunker on the 18th” Rupert Barked back in a slightly higher pitch soaked in irritation.

“I know what I mean Mr Bogey” Eagle snapped back determined to use the name Bogey at every opportunity.

“Well for heavens sake man just declare it GUR… We shan’t bother you at all.”

“GURrrrr” Eagle looked at O’ Par screwing up his face wondering whether this was some new acronym the police were meant to use. He could never keep up.

“Ground under repair” O’ Par confirmed… “it means they won't play from it you know like it’s out of order.”

“Exactly …at least someone knows what they're doing” Mr Bogey mellowed thinking he might be making progress.

“So shall we just leave the forensics team in there while you and your fellow golfers hit balls at them?…. Would you ever cop on” O’ Par stared intently at Bogey until he had to look away.

Rupert Bogey was not used to being spoken to like this…but before he could turn his anger up a notch Eagle raised his own voice, just a notch, and exhaled his frame to its fullest potential. “I am afraid the course is closed until further notice”.

“I know the Commissioner … perhaps I will call him” was all the beleaguered captain could come up with.

“Please do sir” Eagle added more politely …. “Be sure to tell him that you want to play in the same sandpit as a dead body…”

“Bunker, it’s a bloody bunker” Bogey cried out in despair as he turned around purple as a plum … “and you don’t play out of G U R.”

“It’s certainly bloody now Sir” Eagle was quick to respond.

“Well, we are playing I can tell you that much ... even if it has to be on the East Course… though it hasn’t been set up for a qualifier.”

Rupert Bogey was becoming more incensed with each passing second.

"Captain Bogey (Eagle was enjoying this exchange) North, South, East, wherever your compass takes you as long as there are no dead bodies lying in wait feel free to play. We will get you your course back minus the dead body as soon as possible."

Rupert Bogey departed in a hurry disgusted at the interruption to the course schedule.

"Can't we just frame that feckin eejit." Eagle looked at O' Par.

"Tempting Jenny, seriously tempting."

"What an Amadon." Eagle would never tire of the endless supply of put downs that his partner was able to recall at will.

"Jenny … we had 16 booked in earlier for debrief it seems one is missing… so you think you could find out who is missing, where he is and why he isn't here."

"Jaysus you lost one already you gobshite…sure if there was work in the bed you would sleep on the floor". Eagle tried to suppress a smile.

"I have my best person on it now so fuck off". It was important to O' Par to get the last word "You're such a sap … I am not sure you would even work if we put batteries in you."

Eagle knew better than to combat this. Instead, he looked around the room again and began thinking of the puzzle before him… balls he thought. Golf balls. How did it come to this. "Jenny, just one more thing" Eagle called out after her doing his best Lieutenant Columbo impression.

"Who the fuck is Ian Woosnam?"

Chapter 2

The Next Shot

"An interesting thing about golf is that no matter how badly you play, it is always possible to get worse."

Eagle stretched and cricked his neck from left to right. He could already feel the tightness in his body ….and levels of stress rising. Keeping these golfers together in the same room was like herding cats. No sooner had O' Par found the mystery missing 16th man than a new headcount revealed three others had found a way to escape.

"What the fuck is going on sergeant … can't we keep these fuckers in the same room for five minutes so I can tell them what is going to happen now." Eagle didn't quite have steam coming out of his ears but wasn't far short.

O' Par returned and slipped in alongside her boss. "Where did you find him" Eagle nodded to the 16th man who had been escorted back by O' Par. He was a thick set tall bull of a man with dark hair and razor-sharp eyebrows and a slab of a forehead.

"Jaysus Mary and Joseph sure he is what we call at home a dope. You would call him the village idiot.... A dope, an eejit, a gombeen, an amadan, a total gobshite ... he is away with the fairies. Sure yer man that was winning is dead so this fella said he was gonna hit a few balls to loosen up so he was on top of his game...as he was only four shots back like and so now only two ... what with yer man with the flag up his hole out of action". There it was again hole.

"Excuse me?"

"He was acting the maggot ... he thought they were still playing golf today ... just 4 players short and he was getting in some practice as he was confident that he had a chance of winning" O' Par couldn't help but smile. "He asked if tee off had been delayed because of the dead bodies."

"Jenny, we need to speak to this muppet the guys got serial killer written all over him, get him in here and keep him here." Eagle already knew this man wasn't their killer, but he certainly had the physical menace to be of interest and at the very least they needed to keep an eye on this fuckwit for his own safety.

Golf is a game whose aim is to get a very small ball into an even smaller hole with weapons singularly ill-designed for the purpose. That's how Winston Churchill had described it. Eagle contemplated the notion of a ball fitting into an even smaller hole. On this matter perhaps Winston didn't have a clue what he was talking about. Eagle couldn't blame him. Golf was hard to understand. They say in golf the next shot is the most important. It's frivolous soundbites like that which demonstrate just what a bunch of wankers' golfers are according to Eagle. That said, the next stage in the investigation was undoubtedly the most important as far as Eagle was concerned. It was a simple premise really. How to make some sense of what happened here. Simple, if you accept that a game of golf can lead to 4 callous and inexplicably brutal murders.

"Jenny can someone bring those 3 back in here." The recently missing three members of the Society were deep in conversation having made their way out onto the adjacent balcony and had caught Eagles eye. One in particular, a diminutive smartly dressed man was remonstrating with the other two almost pleading his case underneath a sign pointing the way to the Ian Woosnam course. An officer was sent to retrieve them. Eagle got a good look at the guy flapping his arms around. Note to self, diamond tank top.

Four men. Four golfers from the same fourball. Four guys who came away for a weekend of golf and frivolity who were now dead. Something must connect them over and above the fact they knew each other and belonged to the same Society of golfers. They had certainly pissed off someone. There was a very small possibility that the killer was unknown to them. Maybe they stumbled across something, maybe they were in the wrong place, places at the wrong time but it seemed unlikely given the locations and manner of deaths. Of course, there could be a homicidal maniac on the loose. Perhaps someone outside of the group might have been involved but it was hard to escape the notion that one of the 16 remaining golfers who hadn't thus far had a golf ball shoved down their throat, or up their anus, was responsible for the deaths. So, all that remains is to find out what happened and why and who was responsible for the carnage. Or, as Green declared cracking the case before he left the scene, find the sleeve of golf balls with two remaining Pro V1s nestled in and find the killer.

Motive, murder weapon, opportunity. A room full of suspects.

"Jenny, I want to find out more about the dead guys. We need to know who they are, what they did, we need some idea of who knew who, then with this lot", Eagle looked around the room at those gathered, "I want to know who went where and what time last night. We need a timeframe of events. What the hell happened."

O' Par rolled her eyes "On it".

"Let's get this over with and then we can get on to the security cameras." Eagle did his best to sound as sincere as he could. He was addressing a room of gentleman at home listening to speeches. He expressed sorrow for the loss of their friends but explained how important it was that his officers were able to understand what had happened last night. They would need to surrender their clubs briefly and allow forensics to examine clothing and fingernails. We will be as unobtrusive as we possibly can, but each member of the society would need to make a statement to an officer. He understood that they were due to stay at the hotel this evening and it would be helpful if anyone who was not planning on doing so let them know. Jenny whispered "Are you going all Agatha Christie on us Sir."

Jenny's Amadan, or was it dope, raised his hand up and it sent Eagle straight back to the school classroom. "Are we still playing today". He had egg running down his chin and the collar of his polo shirt had collected its fair share of egg yolk too. "Once you have been cleared by forensics and given statements you can do as you please."

And then the diamond tank top took it upon himself to speak to the room with a very soft hint of an accent "I have spoken with our captain and Keith and I feel that in honour of our fallen comrades we should play and get together this evening to pay our respects … as long as the police don't think there is still a lunatic on the loose." This made Eagle's ears prick up. So many things to pick apart. 'Comrades' unusual way to refer to friends. 'Lunatic on the loose'. There was going to be a police presence at the scene for some time to come and it suited Eagle to keep these guys here in one place for as long as he could.

The Amadan gave a little fist pump. Well, there is a least one lunatic on the loose Eagle thought to himself.

Maybe this Ian Woosnam character was a suspect. His name had already popped up several times. Eagle made a note to find out what he could about him when he had time but there was work to do. He wanted to speak to the hotel manager and hotel security about CCTV footage and he wanted to revisit the crime scenes again. Forensics would busy themselves and Jenny could be trusted to have statements done and dusted in an orderly fashion having briefed the officers on specifics that were required.

Eagle made his way out to the reception desk and bumped into the Club Captain who gave him a wide berth. Two members of staff were carrying down a cardboard cut-out hole-in-face wedding portrait that had been used for a wedding fayre the previous day. You know the kind of thing you see at the seaside for a photo opportunity. The bride had a cock and balls drawn on her head and the groom had an ample pair of breasts drawn on and again cock and balls on display. Eagle chuckled to himself. Never not funny he thought, then caught himself before he reached the desk. "What's this" he asked …

"Just one of many things that went missing last night" the receptionist confirmed rolling her eyes much like O' Par had just done. The manner in which he could elicit the same response was phenomenal. Something he had said perhaps. The hotel manager had appeared.

"Actually, I'm the complex manager." He introduced himself to Eagle.

"You're telling me it's certainly complex."

"Well last night was quite raucous. We had our hands full with that lot" he was nodding toward the reception room where the now depleted golf society were.

"So, they were hard work" Eagle played down his interest.

"Nothing we couldn't handle" the hotel manager feigned the faintest of smiles.

"Still haven't found the full-size cut-out of the bride but other than that oh and the, you know, whole incident with the murders and the bodies…"

"The runaway bride" Eagle laughed to himself.

"Yes quite" the complex manager tried to force a more genuine smile.

“Security cameras. I was wondering if we might talk about security cameras..”

“Of course I blame the hole-in-one.” Eagle read the name badge. Jean had exploded into action. She simply couldn’t contain herself.

“What’s that Jean you blame a hole-in-one.”

“Well yes” Jean managed through her layers of make-up. “One of the golfers was celebrating his first ever hole-in-one. He was buying drinks for everyone in the building. It got a bit out of hand.”

“Yes, that will be enough Jean” the complex manager intervened. Eagle read the name badge.. Julian. It would be fair to say that Julian was having a bad day at the office. What with the missing cardboard cut-outs and dead bodies everywhere. Now a hole-in-one was one of the few golfing terms Eagle was acquainted with thanks to a terrible Christmas joke he had once read. It goes like this ‘Question - why did the golfer carry a spare pair of trousers in his golf bag. Answer - in case he got a hole in one. The pen and notepad came out, the famous notepad. He wrote hole-in-one and scrawled a big ‘who’ next to this and added a bigger question mark. A quick double take and he reflected on his notes. They read…

“**golf balls Pro V1s**” underlined and then "hole-in-one! WHO" exclamation mark, "Security Cameras" and "Ian Woosnam"?? Double question mark.

Hole!!! Accent.

Chapter 3

A hole-in-one and one in the hole

"A gimme can be best defined as an agreement between two golfers, neither of whom can putt very well."

"Gimme all you got then" Eagle fired at Jenny O' Par as she joined him an hour or so after the two had gone their separate ways. O' Par was tasked with getting statements, or at least organising the team at her disposal to elicit statements from the nomadic, and as it became increasingly apparent, slightly hungover golfers wandering around the breakfast room like rabbits caught in the headlights. Bringing a semblance of order to the room would be no mean feat. Eagle was going to walk through the crime scenes again, something he liked to do on his own, look at things afresh, utilise perspective, quiet uninterrupted perspective. He was also going to try and get the lowdown on what the cameras caught. If the cameras caught anything that is. Were the bloody cameras even working. These places always gave the impression that every inch of public space was under the watchful eye of Big Brother but the cheapskates never bothered to pay for the coverage they pretended to have.

Eagle greeted O' Par warmly after she finally tracked him down. Julian was about as pleased to see her as he was Eagle lumbering around reception and couldn't wait to send her on her way.

"I assume you have found our killer Jenny and we can all go home".

"Aren't you some dryshite" she shot back "you're as thick as manure and only half as useful."

"What does that even mean" Eagle laughed pretending to be half-offended. After four attempts at the Wi-Fi password Eagle had finally managed to access the complex's Wi-Fi. It was certainly more complex than it needed to be. Why the fuck did they pick a combination of letters, numbers, symbols and then throw in the curveball of upper- and lower-case letters indiscriminately. Luckily attempt four was successful otherwise there may well have been another dead body to deal with. Namely whoever Eagle set eyes on first. He was contemplating launching his phone out of the window into the water feature outside Julian's office. Julian had kindly let Eagle use his own office. Kindly, might not have been the right choice of word. He had no choice really. Julian was having a bad day. He had a full hotel, an unhappy wedding conference organiser and a golf course out of action, oh and not to mention the 4 dead bodies outstaying their welcome to deal with. 4 violently murdered bodies. The last thing he needed was the angry giant lingering around reception talking about dead bodies.

“Actually, let me go first” Eagle interjected and then paused for dramatic effect. “Ok so I don’t think it was Ian Woosnam”. Having managed to get online he had used his extensive research skills and googled Ian Woosnam and read his Wikipedia entry with interest. “Woosnam was the first Welshman to win a Major. Won the Masters. That’s good apparently. Then he had an incident with too many clubs in his bag at the Open Championship in 2001. That is not so good. Received a two-shot penalty, again bad. Now this was the most interesting part. He didn’t sack his caddie. The suspect, a one Miles Byrne. He was meant to count the clubs by all accounts but not sure why the lazy Welsh bastard couldn’t count his own clubs. I thought golfers were good at counting. Apparently, golf is all about counting. You shout Fore, score six and write down five.” Eagle was pleased with his little quip, but O’ Par was unmoved and he continued.

“But anyway, Woosie, that’s this Woosnam guy said his Caddie wouldn’t make the same mistake again, but nevertheless he did sack him a couple of weeks later when he didn’t turn up on time after a night drinking on the town. So, if you are going to tell me one of the victims is a Miles Byrne, we might need to call Woosnam in for questioning, but we can rule him out as a person of interest otherwise”.

“Well aren’t we lucky to have you on our side” Jenny smiled at her boss “and you have even worked out how to use the internet and everything.”

“I also checked his alibi. He was playing a senior event in Spain. Not sure it could have been him.”

“Well, there’s no use boiling your cabbage twice now is there”. This was too much for Eagle.

“OK you win. What you got because the camera coverage is piss poor and at the moment I got nothing of use”.

“I am sure something will pop up. So we have got Tom, Tom, Tom and Michael. Tom O’ Keefe, Tom O’Toole and Tom O’ Shea.”

“Oh!”

“Exactly the three Os and then Michael Flannery is yer man with the flag up his hole.”

“Right Flannery, poor bugger, so what do we know about these 4 together that might give us an idea why they were targeted…”

“You mean quite why they were fecked the way they were”.

“That’s one way of putting it but yeah the three Toms and Michael. How do these things work. Do they play together by chance or like that’s what is agreed. They all know each other but do…” Eagle corrected himself since they had all since expired, “did they like each other.”

"Jaysus Sir that crowd… the four of them had the time of their lives. Apparently, they were having the craic the whole way round. And like when yer man Flannery got his hole-in-one he said it was the best day of his life."

"Ah yes. The hole-in-one. Big deal apparently. Jenny, what do you know about the hole-in-one because my friend Jean from reception has pin-pointed it as the catalyst for a crazy night."

"Well now your man Flannery, flag up the jacksie man, (how could he forget) he got one yesterday. And he was fairly delighted with himself. It's like a big thing. Da got one once back home in Connemara and he didn't stop going on about it for weeks. There's like a plaque on the feckin wall in the club and everything."

"So it's like pretty special."

"Oh yeah …unless your Kim Jong Un."

"Don't tell me he was playing here too" Eagle raised his eyebrows.

"No but sure if he did, he would have got 18 hole-in-ones so it's not quite so special."

Statistically, the chances of an amateur golfer getting a hole-in-one is 12,500 to one. The odds are greatly improved 2,500 to one for a professional. If you were wondering, the chances of two golfers in the same fourball getting a hole-in-one is approximately 17 million to 1. The chances of the same golfer getting two hole-in-ones in the same round are in the region of 67 million to one. Eagle had done his research via an insurance website. It's crazy but hole-in-one insurance was like a thing. He felt much more comfortable and at home with crime statistics. In the UK in 2022 the homicide rate was 11.7 per million population. As for the chances of a fourball being murdered on the same night, well that was entering into the world of the unknown. After dazzling O' Par with his stats he confirmed he got it.

"Hole in-one good thing."

"Well mostly but not everyone was as delighted as yer man Michael from what I heard."

"What did you hear? Jenny get someone to speak to me about what happened yesterday with the hole-in-one."

And that's how it happened. Frank was back.

"Well now Seamus and I were in the fourball with the two young lads. Ballbags well that's not his real name and Blainy. Jaysus those guys can drink. Dear God." Frank was building up a head of steam. "They were feckin drinking like prohibition was on the way…like it was going out of fashion. A shot of Port on every tee … beers on the way round. But like we were behind the guys you know like the guys that" … Pause.

"The dead fourball … Sorry" Eagle helped out apologetically.

"Yeah them. Terrible thing God love em. Now ahead of them would be Tom … (another Tom of course just what was needed). Tom Noonan. He was playing with Brendan, JC and feckin yer man Jed… he's not the full ticket that one… anyway sure we were on the tee watching them play their shots. We had been held up. It was the 7th hole. Michael's lucky number. The other group ahead had stopped to see where the tee shots went coz yer man Tom."

"Which Tom are you referring to now" Eagle asked.

"Noonan." Frank confirmed. "The one that's still alive. Well he had just hit closest to the pin. And we are there having caught them guys up. So we are watching and drinking Port. Jaysus it's mighty stuff. Anyway, doesn't Michael feckin take his swing. Now, I told him well you must have stepped in dog shit on the way over to get that luck. Sure he has a swing, well now the best way to describe it would be that if you ever saw a man trying to strangle a python in a phone box."

This left Eagle doing his best to envisage a man wrestling a python in a phone box…

Frank continued… "and sure didn't he hit this ball off of the toe of the club and it skipped in the bunker then out the bunker rolled up to the flag and hit it like a runaway train. If the flag wasn't there the ball would still be running now but in any events what happens is the ball goes in the hole and your man gets a hole-in-one. Just his lucky day I suppose."

"Hmmm!" Eagle let that hang in the air and couldn't help but mention that "Well not quite his lucky day." I suppose given that it ended up with him being clubbed to death, stripped and with a flagpole up his arse? In reality, he stopped at the point where he had highlighted it wasn't quite his lucky day. That's quite a vivid depiction Eagle and O' Par were captivated.

"And what then." O' Par was first to respond.

"Ah yeah, well didn't Michael burst into tears. He couldn't believe it. He was whooping like a banshee." Frank stops to lick his lips. "We cracked open more beers and didn't Michael shake up the tin and spray it round like he was celebrating a podium celebration."

"So it's just a happy thing. A magnificent sporting achievement. Harmless." Eagle was fishing.

"I guess. Tom…Tom Noonan, was a little annoyed like because he had hit a lovely 8 iron to within two foot of the hole and then yer man just feckin hit a shot you know a shit shot that worked. That's golf like. It's better to be a lucky golfer than a good one."

And with that Frank puffed out his cheeks and took a moment to pause and reflect.

“That was just Michael. He was full of shit. He said he definitely meant to play a low runner into the green. Imagine.”

"But why wasn’t Tom number 4 pleased.” Eagle still didn’t fully understand.

“Well Tom, Tom Noonan was annoyed because it meant Michael won the nearest the pin prizes. I mean you can’t get much closer than in the hole and so Michael won a nice bottle of whiskey and two sleeves of golf balls. Pro V1s.” There it was again. The Pro V1s.

“Tom said they were wasted on Michael because they would only end up in the woods. But Michael bought everyone in the clubhouse a drink. And it didn’t stop. The drinks were flowing. He was delighted.”

Eagle’s mind was running away with itself. “So the guy who got the hole in one then got one in the hole”. Technically two in the hole what with first a golf ball shoved up his backside and then the positioning of the flag. Eagle didn’t mean to talk aloud and so immediately moved on to consider the statistics involved. How many golfers die on the day they got a hole in one. How many were murdered. How many golfers celebrating a hole in one ended up face down in the sandpit, sorry bunker, he corrected himself, butt naked with their brains smashed in and a flag up their arse for good measure.

Chapter 4

Golf on the Moon

"If profanity influenced the flight of the ball, the game of golf would be played far better than it is."

"Feck. It's all a bit of a bollox."

With Frank only to keen to offer his assistance should they need his help with anything else Eagle thanked him once again for his help before politely sending him on his way. Like his fellow golfers he had given a statement and was awaiting the release of his clubs. Forensics had been using infrared handheld technology to determine whether any of the clubs belonging to the collective group displayed signs, or traces to be more precise, of blood. In other words, was there a potential murder weapon in any of the golf bags gathered in the room. Needless to say, if this was the case then it greatly increased the chances of one of the Birchgrove Irish golf Society being a killer. No one had wanted to come out and say it but sometimes it's what is not said that can carry greater poignancy. Everyone had done as they were told and given up their clubs. And the clubs belonging to the deceased men had also been located.

The aim for the Society was to make a rescheduled tee time post lunch. By this time Captain Bogey and his fellow competitors would have been well on their way for the qualifier on the East Course. Frank was keen to return to the group. Once Eagle was sure Frank was out of earshot he casually asked "Which one is Tom Noonan."

"He is yer man that stood up in the diamond tank top."

Eagle couldn't help showing a sudden surge of interest, a flicker of enthusiasm, a tell-tale twitch of the eyes, an unwanted bolt of energy that made the muscles in his neck move slight quicker than they were used to and certainly quicker than O' Par was accustomed to seeing in her boss. He tried to stop himself but he knew it was too late.

O' Par looked at him "What's the story … you can't hide that look from me. You have a bad dose of looking pleased with yourself."

"It's nothing" he held his hands up.

"I swear I will eat the head off you if you don't tell me what you're thinking."

Again, such a way with words. Eagle pondered whether to let her know what he was thinking. It was always better to have her on your side and so he just came out with it.

"It's just he stood out to me. He went AWOL on the balcony and I saw him holding court with two other chaps. There was something about it that didn't quite blend in with the environment. You know, given the circumstances. Murder. Dead bodies. Loss of friends. It seemed heated I guess." Eagle stroked his non-existent beard.

"Then I hear him harping on about fallen comrades… I don't know." He took a sharp intake of breath. "I need a good cup of tea." Anything to get rid of the engine oil coffee he had on route from the petrol garage.

"And why was he so pissed at his mates' good fortune. It's not every day you get a hole-in-one… unless your Kim Jong Un…apparently."

"Well maybe they're not mates" O' Par chipped in.

"Exactly…maybe there not."

"Agh would you cop on. No one is gonna murder 4 people because they missed out on a bottle of whiskey and some shitty golf balls."

"You heard Green… there not shitty golf balls. The best money can buy."

With his Wi-Fi access secured Eagle had already googled Pro V1 golf balls and was mildly, and only mildly amused at coming across a meme, don't look so surprised, Eagle wasn't that out of touch, anyway this meme had a guy abseiling down the edge of a cliff and there was a guy looking down at him shouting 'Leave it. Save yourself it's not worth it'. And the guy half-way down the cliff was reaching out for a little white golf ball on the edge of a sharp drop and his reply was 'You don't understand it's a Pro V1.'

"Nik" whenever Jenny O' Par addressed him by his first name, he knew he was in trouble "I am telling you no one, not even a sociopathic maniac is gonna kill anyone over a golf ball. Let alone kill four people over a feckin pack of golf balls."

"Two sleeves of golf balls Jenny."

Eagle was keen not to read too much into it, but Tom Noonan was certainly someone he wanted to know more about.

The real problem of course was that at this stage they knew very little about the 4 deceased men. Equally, when it came to considering a list of suspects, they also knew very little about their contemporaries. A group of 20 had arrived. They were now down to 16 and while they couldn't rule out foul play from an outsider, there was something incredibly brutal and vindictive about the demise of these men and that spoke familiarity. It suggested a personal vendetta. It suggested the kind of anger and rage that can only be reserved for a person or persons known to the perpetrator. At least that is what Eagle believed.

It was early stages. The primary focus at the outset of any investigation was fact building and evidence gathering. Piece the pieces together. Who is involved and who is not part of the story. Eagle was keen to find out as much as he could about the golf society and its members and he was relying on his team to acquaint themselves and fill him on the circumstances surrounding the deaths, the timeframe and as he would label them for ease at this point in time the persons of interest, namely the members of the Birchgrove Irish Golf Society, or to put it another way, the suspects. There were other parties to consider of course. Hotel guests of which there were too many to contemplate, hotel staff, the Greenkeeper who discovered the first body, the chamber maid who discovered the two bodies in room 13, but this was largely just unwanted noise as far as Eagle was concerned at this stage.

Before he returned to touch base with the team taking the statements, he still needed to revisit the crime scenes and it seemed obvious to start with the most brutal of the murders and as it happens closest to the office where Eagle was situated, which was that of Michael Flannery who lay in the sandpit, make that bunker, on the 18th hole.

Flannery also happened to be the first body discovered earlier that morning, and this had happened almost simultaneously from two contrasting views. As one of the breakfast maids opened the curtains to open up the view looking out of the breakfast room onto the signature hole at the Chorus Hills golf and country club a lone greenkeeper approached the 18th from the fairway riding on a sit on lawn mower. It was a little before 6.30am and the sun was shining and reflecting off the morning dew clinging to the 18th Green. The Sun was shining and the Moon was also still visible, in more ways than one.

Incidentally golf was the first sport played on the Moon. Shortly before leaving the surface of the moon on February 6th, 1971,

Apollo 14 Commander and golfer Alan Shepard swung at two golf balls with a custom made 6-iron. The maid, a young 17-year-old girl, Grace, and greenkeeper, coincidentally another Alan, though not a Shepherd, were each faced with a different kind of moon. A pale white moon, the backside belonging to Michael Flannery. It was, for both of them, a first, a first discovery of a of dead body. The maid had let out a scream. Not only could she see Michael's pale bottom she could also see what looked like a significant injury to his head which seemed to be misshapen and bloody. There was a magpie pecking at him. Alan, the greenkeeper could be forgiven at first for thinking he had stumbled upon a pissed-up golfer sleeping it off in the bunker. Perhaps stripped naked and left face down to sleep it off. What a night he must have had. As Alan got closer to the green, the scene became more disturbing. The flag from the 18th green had been positioned between the sleeping golfer's legs and was earmarking his naked butt. Perhaps as some kind of joke. But when he saw the magpie digging into the sleeping guys head Alan became fully aware that this was no sleeping golfer. Out of a sense of respect he shooed the bird away and did his best to compose himself and call the police. The pro shop wouldn't even open for another 30 minutes. He motioned towards the breakfast room miming towards the maid. It took a few moments for her to understand and draw the curtains.

And the 18th Greenside bunker was where Eagle was headed. His SIO, Jenny O' Par was herself returning to the reception room to check on the progress of the response team and to pin down someone more to the point than Frank, to make sense of yesterday's order of events. The guy called Keith. It was his Captain's Away Weekend. So perhaps as the organiser he could take charge and run her through the events of yesterday. The golf and well... the after party. Eagle had barely made it out of the office, Julian's office, when Julian appeared. He looked even more dishevelled and stressed than he had been earlier, but he tried to greet Eagle with a smile and handed over the bookings summary list for the Birchgrove Irish Golf Society. "Thanks" Eagle offered trying not to show any annoyance at another distraction from his destination.

Although not one for multi-tasking, he could at least walk and read on the way, or attempt to read. He briefly stopped in his tracks to check the info he had before his was correct. Party of 21.... He read on. Ten double rooms with surnames listed. And one Single room. Name Hanlan. Where has 21 come from. If four are dead. 16 left in the room. One is missing. The notepad came out.

Chapter 5

Discontent and the Tik Tok Superstar

"A good drive on the 18th hole has stopped many a golfer from giving up the game."

Alan's drive down to the 18th green earlier that morning culminated in the discovery of the lifeless body of Michael Flannery and the image of a magpie scavenging at the poor fella's head was not one he would easily forget. The greenkeeper was able to confirm that after calling the police and ambulance services he contacted reception to let them know about his gruesome discovery. The pro shop was closed but he had messaged his fellow green keeping staff and the pro shop to let them know about the discovery and to get the Woosnam course closed off. He had waited around primarily to protect the body from the magpie. He had eventually plucked up the courage to approach the body, get close enough to reach over and feel for a pulse. His search for a sign of life was half hearted. The mess in his head and vampire bird well that had told him all he needed to know. There was no one else around on the course. He had tried not to disturb the body notwithstanding the urge to remove the flag. The footsteps evident in the bunker had been there since Alan's arrival and were not his. He had made a small imprint where he placed his front foot on tiptoes as he leant over as close as he dare get to check for life. Alan was not a suspect.

Golf has long been considered an acceptable way of avoiding responsibilities. In 1457 golf was banned in Scotland by King James II who was concerned that at a time when Scotland was at war too many military personnel were distracted by the game of golf. Eagle couldn't help but be distracted by the serene beauty of the view around him as he looked back down the fairway to the 18th tee and then back at the sheer horror of the chaos in the sand behind him. Maybe the footprint would be the answer.

Lighting other than some fairy lights on the bridge across the moat protecting the 18th Green was scarce. There was, or at least had been, solar powered sensory lighting around the green itself, Alan had told Eagle this was to keep the deer from wandering into the greens and ruining them. But this lighting which was made to blend in by looking like stones had all been removed. The solar power stone lighting units had been thrown into the water surrounding the green. They had been found by the two frogmen scouring the moat surrounding the 18th green for signs of a murder weapon. A stray golf club at best guess. Something in the curvature of the injuries sustained by all four men had convinced the Pathologist that this was likely, and Green was as familiar with a golf club in his hand, as he was with a scalpel and the postmortem table, but he was keeping an open mind nevertheless. The nod from Green was enough to convince Eagle that they were looking for a golf club as the murder weapon.

There was little else to suggest that the killer or the victim had been seen in the darkness. The only camera footage would have been via the main exit and while it would be checked thoroughly Eagle was not hopeful of capturing anything significant. By all accounts the hot weather had meant the patio doors leading out to the veranda had been open all evening.

The forensics response team were preparing to move the body. It had been made a priority given its location and exposure. This was Eagles cue to move on and venture back inside and visit the other two crime scenes beginning with room 13. He needed to speak with O' Par first and find out what was going on with the numbers. He looked at the document in his hand. A confirmation list of the booking. 11 rooms. Not ten. And 21 names. Not twenty but 21. He messaged Jenny.

‘On way back. 21 golfers not 20!!! Who is our mystery golfer?’

O’ Par greeted Eagle as he marched into the reception room parting two officers stood guard at the doorway as he stomped his way towards her.

“Would you stop with the exclamation marks” she raised her eyes as she spoke.

“Do you know Jenny”, she secretly liked it when he called her Jenny rather than O’ Par partly because she never heard him address anyone else by their first name. “Sigmund Freud said that the Irish are one race for whom psychoanalysis is of no use whatsoever.”

“Ah stop sure wasn’t he too busy sleeping with his Mammy to visit us or something.”

Eagle shook his head. He would never get the better of her and there was no point trying.

“What’s going on with the numbers. What are we missing.”

“We” O’ Par retorted at a pitch higher than Eagle was accustomed to hearing from her before returning to her usual calm self, “we are missing nothing. You, (again a slight change of pitch) well you were too busy trying to pin the murders on a wee Welsh Guy with an alibi.” There was a constant low distracting humming from the conversations going on in the room.

"We have a non-golfer in the mix. A kinda PA type who is sharing a room with err a golfer..."

"Have I missed something. Did Tiger Woods turn up to keep an eye on things."

"What are you're shite-ing on about." Eagle knew better than to interrupt so waited for O' Par to continue. He often found that if he left it long enough his SIO usually came up with the answer he was after, always delivered in her own unique way.

"We can do better than Tiger Woods." She led him back out into the corridor away from the noise. "These guys..." she nodded towards the room they had just escaped from.... "One of their members is a bit of a celeb."

"Go on."

"Grandad Gabe ... Triple G, Golfing Grandad Gabe" ... Eagle tried his best not to look completely out of the loop. O' Par was not one to be easily fooled.

"Tik Tok Sir"...

"Yeah the clock is ticking Jenny ... I still don't know who the fuck Grandad Gabe is... Triple G. Is he a wrestler or something" Eagle asked optimistically.

“Nada Tik Tok you shitehawk. He is a Tik ToK superstar. “Golfing Grandad Gabe. 8 million followers. Tell me you know what the feck Tik Tok is.”

Eagle had heard of it. “I know of it. Social media. Instagram, Facebook and Tickety Tok…all the rage…amongst young people… stupid dances. My nephew has shown me. Even tried to get me to do a stupid dance with him and his sister but as for Grandads well that’s a new one on me.”

“Tickety Tok indeed, well I would love to see that video” O’ Par scoffed.

Eagle pretended to be offended.

“Compared to this Grandad” awkward pause … “Well, Jaysus, Triple G makes you look positively ancient” O’ Par laughed.

“So this guy… Triple G” this time Eagle shook his head in disbelief, “Tik Tok Superstar… he is here but didn’t play golf.”

“No that’s the thing. He plays golf. He is part of the Society. One of the founding members in fact. But like now he is a big deal so he came with his PA. They were planning some content across the weekend for his followers. It’s a full-time job keeping those followers happy. That’s where 21 comes in.”

“Followers” it reminded Eagle of a cult for some reason.

"Gabriel, that's Gabe he shared a room with his PA, a guy called Daniel. And one of the other guys an old boy. Pat, He had his own room. Terrible snorer apparently."

Eagle could sympathise. He suffered from the same affliction, especially when he was particularly tired or if he had enjoyed a few pints. He put that down as the main reason for ruining his last meaningful relationship. Nothing to do with the job and his constant disappearing acts and inability to ever be where he said he would be on time.

Eagle was thinking on his feet. He had no other choice since they were stood in the hallway. Did this change anything? Well, he had one guy potentially on his own in a room perhaps without an alibi for his movements. That guy was also 84 years of age and according to O' Par 'an absolute dote'. A sweetheart. 'A gentleman.' Added to the party was a non-golfer. A personal assistant to an internet sensation. A Tik Tok superstar. One of the most famous Grandads in the country by all accounts. Maybe the world. He had even been on several daytime shows talking about his sudden stardom and his love of golf and hip-hop music which spawned his fusion Tik Tok routines giving golf tips and fashion advice to hip hop tracks. Christ, where do they get these ideas from. Eagle made a note to find a quiet corner and watch a few reels, yeah reels, it was all coming back to him now. He was as hip as any Gangster Grandad in plus fours. Really, Triple G. At his age he should be thinking hip replacement rather than hip hop. Eagle was pleased with that one and chortled to himself. Fame can sometimes change people but doesn't necessarily make them any more likely to kill. So Triple G would need to be treated the same as everyone else and his assistant, well he would need to make himself known and the team would have to have him account for his whereabouts the same as the rest of the party.

Eagle looked up at O' Par. She already knew what he was thinking. "The assistant is on his way down to join us and Gabriel, has already given a statement."

"Ok good." Eagle thought aloud "I think we need to check in with the homicide handbook and check we are ticking all the boxes."

Eagle and his senior investigating officer both looked up at the same time as there was movement ahead of them.

Swaggering towards them in a dark hoodie, ripped jeans with headphones on and carrying a phone in one hand and looking at a laptop in the other a young man in his twenties swayed down the corridor as if in his own little world. Not a care about him thought O' Par. As he got closer Eagle spotted that he was wearing a hoodie with a branded Triple G lightning logo embossed in fluorescent colours in contrast to the blackness of the rest of the material. This must be the PA he thought, then as an afterthought branded merchandise. People will buy anything won't they. Having said that he quite liked the colours of the logo.

Chapter 6

93 over par and the Harlem Shake

"Golf... is the infallible test. The man who can go into a patch of rough alone, with the knowledge that only God is watching him, and play his ball where it lies, is the man who will serve you faithfully and well."

Gabriel, Grandad Gabe, Golfing Grandad Gabe, Triple G, also known within the Society as TikTok, something which made him uncomfortable, well Eagle was only going to call him Gabriel, ok maybe Gabe because that's how he liked to be addressed, couldn't speak highly enough of Daniel. A clever kid. Not a kid. 25. But faithful and couldn't do enough for you. He had guided Gabe, all the way through his Tik Tok journey. He is sound. Solid. Reliable. Full of ideas. Kind. Generous. Creative. Faithful. There it was faithful again. Gabriel clearly liked the man. Eagle and O' Par had no choice but to play it as it lay. Gabriel had sung his young assistant's praises, but they were going to find out for themselves what Daniel had to say about himself.

Let's get this straight Eagle thought, he is not a kid. He is a man. 25 years old. Sure, he dressed like a kid. He is not bad looking at all O' Par has noticed… for someone barely out of school. Daniel James, 25 years old, with his blond tousled hair slightly wavy at the front reaching up into a peaked quiff had sat himself away from the rest of the group. He was busy tapping away on his laptop, while also looking at his phone and interchangeably flicking between the two devices. Eagle looked on in unveiled disgust. As someone who often took minutes to compile and send a text message he despised how easy young people, not even young people, other people made communicating electronically look so easy.

They introduced themselves and sat across from him. He knew he needed to give a statement and run through the events of the previous evening. Daniel James wasn't sure how much help he could be. He didn't know these guys really and had been busy shut away working on content to go live but he immediately gave them his full attention. Closed his laptop and put his phone away. "I'm all yours" he flashed a smile. It was brief but friendly.

"Quite a shock I suppose" Eagle spoke first.

"Yeah. I am not quite sure how we are going to play it. We have promised some tips from the course. Built it up. Not sure we will use any of it now."

Eagle noted that his first response was for the content and the job in hand and not related to the tragic loss of lives.

"I feel really bad for Gabe. He loves these guys. Obviously it's tragic and all that. Been playing with them for years. Less so recently as he doesn't have the time." Almost to fill the silence that permeated the room Daniel James continued "I know he was really looking forward to this weekend. Catching up with them." Both officers sat with their eyes affixed on him. If he felt a little uneasy, he tried not to show it. O' Par offered him some encouragement.

"It's sad alright." She pretended to consult her notes, a trick she had picked up from Eagle. If people think something is written down, then it is set in stone. "Gabe said you didn't join them last night for dinner."

Without hesitation Daniel James answered her "No I had a couple of drinks with the guys to be sociable. Then I walked around the Complex, checking out the best spots for some footage today. Then I had to get back finish editing a couple of things and send them back to the office so that the final reels could be approved."

This time it was Eagles tutn to consult his real notebook but imaginary notes. "What time were you back in the room."

"Probably by 9… I finished editing by 11 and sent the pre-production clips off to the office. Got the green light and went live a few minutes later. I must have been asleep when Gabe came up to bed."

O' Par jumped in. "Daniel, can we see the latest content. The videos published last night". Daniel was happy to oblige and opened up his laptop which brought him to Triple Gs profile straight away Golfing Grandad Gabe.

Eagle braced himself. First up Daniel was only too pleased to introduce the outfit change transition trend and a video of Gabriel stood on the bridge. Eagle recognised the location immediately. The signature hole, the 18th, the bridge over the moat and a little further along the bunker and final resting place of Michael Flannery. Gabe was posing and dancing, well, moving in any case, possibly imitating what Eagle might loosely identify as a gangster pose. The camera would take in the outfit and then then a golf ball would fill the screen, suddenly flash up like it was going to hit the screen and immediately cut to Gabe who would be wearing a different outfit. Then the same flash and a third outfit and finally a fourth. Each transition included an additional accessory, golf club, hat, umbrella. There was a different track accompanying each outfit. All by artists Eagle had never heard of or if he had, he had put the knowledge well and truly out of his mind.

Eagle was trying to take it all in. But he had learnt something new at least. He now knew what the outfit change transition trend was, and he felt all the better for it. Daniel James was clearly pleased with the end result. It had already been viewed 757,000 times.

“We did several of those” Daniel James proudly announced…. “We spiced it up with big gold chains but it’s to promote Gabe’s new line of golf clothing and particularly the golf hoodies aimed at the younger golfer”. He was on a roll so O’ Par gently stopped Eagle from intervening.

“We took a lot of footage as we got an interesting collab coming up with one of the guys from One Direction… where Gabe and he will be wearing the same outfits in synchronised transitions. Hopefully it will be sic.”

One direction. Yeah, I have heard of them Eagle thought to himself then couldn’t prevent himself from speaking aloud “sick… why would you want to be sick…”

“You are an awful Amadan… sick is like mint … you know it means good…”

“Well not where I am from Jenny” Eagle pretended to be hurt by the rebuke.

“And what’s this one” Eagle asked pointing to the next picture underneath.”

“This is Gabe on the 1st tee doing a hip hop dance called the Harlem Shake, well actually it’s the Harlem Shake, then the Electric Slide and finally the Pop and Lock.”

“Good Lord” Eagle couldn’t help himself.

“It’s a warmup routine to then make sure when he hits the ball he finishes the shot by getting the hips through the ball.”

O’ Par held her hand out to stop Eagle commenting.

“The bling belt … that is to make sure the buckle hits the imaginary wall.” Daniel James was looking delighted. “Genuine tip, you see how he finishes the shot with the buckle facing down the fairway.”

“If you say so” Eagle couldn’t resist as the text ran across the screen explaining the tip. At least he recognised the track this time. “Rappers Delight by the Sugarhill gang” and with that Eagle broke into a couple of ill-advised lines of song.

Daniel and Jenny both looked up at the burly detective who looked like he had just won the lottery.

“Jeez that’s desperate Sir.” O’ Par cut him down. Just the 500,000 views of this one.

For a brief moment Eagle wished the room would open up and swallow him whole before composing himself.

This time it was Eagles turn to use his name “So Daniel how do you know Gabriel.”

“Well, I discovered him.”

This elicited a laugh from Eagle. “Come on. How do you discover a 70-year-old man.”

“That is I guess I mean I discovered his Tik Tok persona. Let me explain.”

“12 months ago, I was working on a podcast ‘the Bogeyman’. It’s a golf themed podcast and YouTube channel. They review courses, clubs, tech. A couple of ex journeymen pros. Light-hearted. It’s fun. They knew nothing about editing, or publishing videos….. so I helped them out and eventually worked full time for them.”

“Are you a golfer” Eagle blurted out.

“Well, they say never give a sword to a man who can’t dance.”

O’ Par thought nice answer… Eagle wasn’t happy with the answer. “Sorry, you play golf or not.”

“I did” Daniel offered. “I should say I have been a dancer and a golfer and choreography is kind of my thing. I lost interest in golf and became interested in film and photography … anyway.. as for Gabe. What do you want to know.” Daniel James shrugged nonchalantly.

“Everything” was O’ Par’s answer.

"Strap yourself in." O' Par was warming to this young man all the time. He didn't speak like the men of a similar age that she met. Well, when she said met, she meant contacted online and occasionally, very occasionally, met.

"Mike Reasor". Daniel James offered up the name. "I guess it's all his fault. That's why our paths crossed." He has the attention of both officers. "I am working on the podcast. The guys ask me to research worst scores. You know worst moments for pros. They are comparing golf to other sports and looking at low points and how athletes come back from … well adversity."

PC irons a keen golfer has overheard and has tip toed ever so slightly closer. Intrigued.

"And so, we do this one show called 93 over par. It's about one particular golfer. Mike Reasor. He happens to hold the unfortunate tag of the highest score in a PGA Tour event." Both detectives are giving their full attention.

"This guy, well the evening before the 3rd round of the 1974 Tallahassee Open, He falls off a horse. He damages the ligaments in his left shoulder…..but," Daniel is enjoying his moment and is a good storyteller. Clearly bright and has a head for retaining information… "But he needs to finish the tournament to retain his exemption for the upcoming Byron Nelson Golf Classic. Golf, at the elite level, is essentially about starts and chances to play in other events and make money. So as a result, he had to play on even though he is badly injured. Reasor carries on swinging a 5-iron one-handed the whole round. After the longest day of his professional career, he cards a 123 for a score of +51".

Even Eagle knows this is a lot of shots and unlikely to win any tournament.

"He soldiered on and finished the tournament, shooting a +42, 114 in the final round. After 72 holes, his total was 93 over par."

"Brutal" Jenny adds.

"The point is he carries on. All that matters is finishing. Seeing the journey out."

"Ok but forgive me Daniel, what is the point you're making."

O' Par shot her boss a look. It told him she thought that was rude. She was enjoying the story and the point was coming. She was amazed at how impatient he could be.

"Well, I do the research and we looked at similar stories in other sports and particularly in golf we drew on the whole, what keeps people coming back angle. You know, the hackers. Golf is a super easy game, it's just hard to play."

O' Par could tell Daniel James was building up to something. Her boss had begun to look less irritated and was paying attention again. He was a keen sportsman after all. Just not a golfer.

"Mick and Nate, the guys behind the podcast, they are ex pros, and they had a theory that the less skilled the player, the more likely he is to share his ideas about the golf swing. I set about debunking that myth and I came across Gabe. He was doing little videos inspired by his 16-year-old granddaughter. Offering tips but they were funny. She would appear in them alongside him sometimes and she would sometimes add music, funny voice overs and sort of well you know, pimp him up a bit, you know make him look bad ass. The thing that really got me is that she would try and teach him a dance. He would make a right mess of it but give it his all. And these got the most views. This Golfing Grandad already had 50,000 followers."

Eagle was expecting, demanding more so asked for more simply with his hands.

"Gabe and I hit it off. He helped me with the show. Made a cameo appearance. Got some more traction. In return I helped him out with some content and things went a bit crazy. I got him to reach out to the world of pro golf with a particular video, a kind of Happy Gilmore thing", Eagle was lost, O' Par had seen the film so was vaguely onboard. "It went viral, we had some of the American Pros commenting on it, Big Phil, John Daley, Bryson challenged Gabe to a long drive comp, and then Tiger even gave him a mention. Christ, Paige Spiranic loved it.. she is a big deal. Declared her love for Grandad Gabe."

Eagle was lost but doing his best to follow and make notes.

Daniel James wasn't finished "Former Pro. Lots of followers. If you check her out you will understand. Anyway, the two of us both got signed up as a team with a management company and … the rest is history."

"So here we are."

"Here we are." Daniel agreed.

"93 Over Par."

"You think you could beat that Sir" O' Par threw it out there.

Eagle let out a deep breath "never give a sword to a man who can't dance or a golf club to a man who can't play golf".

"One more question for now Mr James, does Gabe enjoy what he is doing. Does he enjoy being Triple G".

"I think you would need to ask him. I think he loves it some of the time and feels a little awkward at other times".

"Thanks a million Daniel. That will be all for now" O' Par was genuinely appreciative of his time. "Probably best if you don't post, publish anything else for the time being."

“Of course” Daniel James nodded. “One thing I do know is Gabe…. he is not your killer.”

Eagle offered his thanks too and was about to get up but then had a thought that stopped him in his flow. “One more thing Daniel” oh God O’ Par though Columbo is back. “You got lots of footage on the 1st before the Society went off rampaging on the course. You mentioned it was a bit chaotic.” Daniel nodded. “Could we see it, what you recorded I mean.”

Chapter 7

One too many

"As you walk down the fairway of life you must smell the roses, for you only get to play one round."

Gabriel Dormey was a rejuvenated man. You only had one shot at life and he was going to live the best life he could. He had always been a family Man. He had always been a happy soul or so he thought and then boom. Suddenly it happened. Life caught up on him. While he was looking the other way, it crept up without wanting and scared the living shit out of him by suddenly tapping him on the shoulder and asking what next.

Gabriel wasn't ill or anything. His health, touch wood, had always been pretty good. He liked a drink but didn't drink excessively. He ate well. Tried to limit his intake of red meat. Eat plenty of veg and also fish. That was the key. Fish, it was food for the brain. But work, even though he didn't enjoy it well it gave him structure. It meant that his free time wasn't enough to do all the things he wanted to do. But then, in a click of the fingers, he had more free time than he could ever fill. No schedule. No get up time. No time to leave the house. No time to escape the traffic. In fact, what he did have was time. More time than he could ever need. His morning cup of tea turned into two cups and then another and he waited to be told what the plan for the day was. The dog was knocking on 15 years old and at best would walk to the end of the road and back. Retirement was dull.

Becoming Triple G had given him new impetus. A new meaning. A new purpose. Somehow life before had become stale. He stopped enjoying his regular golf. He had stopped enjoying dance classes with his wife of near 50 years. After retiring he didn't really know who he was anymore, what he was, where he fitted in, what he was meant to do with his time. Then his granddaughter Eva who meant the absolute world to him had shown him some dance routines she had put together for her Tik Tok. He didn't really understand what he was seeing but she opened up a world that kept him captivated for hours as one reel led to another and then another.

Eva adores her grandfather as much as he adored her and seeing him struggling even if no one else could see what she could, she tapped into his fun side. She used his love of golf and their joint love of dance to make him happy, make him laugh and film something that she would have to remember him by. Her own father had died young and she had barley any photos of the two together and certainly nothing on video. Before she had even realised what she was doing Eva had created a persona for him. An account. A new profile. An online presence. He began to look forward to each morning. A debrief about what they might do. A golf tip from him and a dance and track from her. Combining the two was always a lot of fun.

He loved reading the comments and the love and wishes that their clips attracted. Gabe played by the rules though and artistic integrity was everything. He made sure he knew what Eva was making him do and why. Then, he got contacted by this guy who was a walking encyclopaedia on golf. Right up his street. A young lad. Can't have been much older than Eva though he was older than he looked. And again boom.. he was signed to a social media influencing management company and he had a million followers then 2, then 5, and now 8 million. He had companies falling over themselves to pay him to endorse products. Celebs wanting to link up… what the actual feck. Gabe couldn't believe what was happening.

As you walk down the fairway of life you must smell the roses, for you only get to play one round. Gabe was playing his round and was determined to play it like it was his last.

The problem was he had a dark secret. A terrible secret. He had one too many. Not just drinks that evening. He had let his guard down and was pleased to catch up with the guys. But he had only realised when he moved his clubs returning to his room that he had a club too many in his bag. He had done a Woosnam. Daniel had given him a new driver to use on the first and he had put it back in the bag rather than hand it back to Daniel before he set off on his round with the guys. What a dilemma. He always played by the rule, what if this led to cheating claims, what if some eagle-eyed spectator picked up on it… could it ruin everything… **One too many**.

Chapter 8

Does your husband play

"A ball you can see in the rough from 50 yards away is not yours."

You really do have to take the rough with the smooth. This is what Tom Noonan thought to himself as he tried to do the calculations.

He had been nervous at first about putting himself forward but was relieved to hear that the consensus was that his time had come. At least that was what he had been told. So he had made his play for the role of Captain. It was his time. He was ready. And looking forward to it. Weighing up the number of members, those that had done the role before, those that hadn't, those that could do it and those that wanted it, and well it looked as though it was his time.

Do you want it Tom, he asked himself. It's yours. He had to put himself forward. So he did. It was a sure thing. A cert. A formality. A few days after the Outgoing captains away weekend the group would gather and sort out the formalities for the following year including the captaincy. It had been a tough year. He was not one to talk about his problems and in any case things were on the up. He had lost someone close to him and it had taken time to deal with that. He had suffered from depression, anxiety and this had manifested itself by instilling an inordinate amount of self-doubt that permeated every decision he had to make. The Captaincy had given him a target and focused his attention and strengthened his resolve to take the bull by the horns and not just let life happen around him.

That was until Michael Flannery decided to interfere and do what he did best, make himself a nuisance. Flannery had decided that he would also put himself up for Captain. Tom Noonan was sure that his former business partners primary motive, possibly only motive, for throwing his hat into the ring was to piss him off. The sure thing was now a two-horse race. Tom was going to make sure there was only one winner. Flannery was flash. He would try and buy favour. But he was also an awful eejit. Tom was the safe pair of hands. He was pretty sure that he was at least a couple of votes to the good.

"Does your husband play" … those words.. that group and the humiliation. Christ he would have wrapped his club round Flannery's head there and then if he could. Thinking back to it he had handled the situation quite well. But in the cold light of day given all that had happened the mutterings he had uttered at the time and then in the bar after could have been misread. Misinterpreted. That aside, he didn't want any real harm to come to his old friend. No matter how much they clashed the two had long since put aside their differences.

When it became too much to continue working with each other, they split the clients and jobs and went their separate ways. Each party claiming to be the biggest concreting firm in the south of England. They remained pals. They just couldn't work together. One being so meticulous about every detail and the other Michael Flannery always chancing his arm, flashing a smile and always saying yes. Yes, to every job, to every deadline. Tom couldn't work like that anymore. Their differing personalities had cemented their separation. No hard feelings. His old business partner had a knack for winding him up and yes it was true that he had often threatened violence against him but always in jest. He was the cranky straight man. The serious one. Michael was the loud brash joker. He never thought it would end like this though for Michael. Even if he was trying to steal the Captaincy from Tom. Even if he was trying to steal two of his workforce. Yes, that's right. Tom Noonan wasn't born yesterday. He knew what he was up to. Could the two Toms be trusted. His two Toms. One thing was for sure O'Toole and O' Shea had no idea that their boss knew treachery was afoot. Flannery hadn't approached them himself. He left that to O'Keefe his little monkey sidekick.

There was a lot that Tom Noonan knew that others didn't. He caught himself daydreaming before he regained his composure. Tom Noonan was sure that the big guy, the detective, knew something. He wouldn't take his eyes off him.

Little more than 24 hours earlier, the Society had gathered, been allocated their playing groups for the day over a late breakfast. It was at breakfast that Flannery had declared he was going to run for Captain. A little friendly competition he had laughed through a mouthful of bread, bacon, sausage and egg swimming in ketchup. The big Oaf. No decorum. No style. Just bulldozing and joking his way through life.

So it was that feckin fool Flannery who had stopped the guys from telling him he had teed it up on the wrong tees. Usually, the ladies' tees would be on a completely different tee box. In fact, most clubs had already done away with the distinction ladies' tees. It was all done on ability and distance now. After waiting around on the 1st for so long the guys in front had taken an age to move on, mainly because TikTok had been filming, dancing around on the 1st like some feckin Jack in a box. Tom Noonan didn't quite get what Gabe was doing and more to the point why.

But it was Flannery who had orchestrated it so that Tom played first with their bags placed alongside the front tees at the front of the tee box and then he asked the other three if they would prefer to play off the Mens tees. To make matters worse, Tom's shot had clipped the trees on the left and only just stayed in bounds by the skin of its teeth.

Then to rub salt into the wounds that little fecker Tom O Keefe, Flannery's sidekick, pipes up with the classic .. "Does your husband play" comment. Ha feckin ha. Very funny you little prick.

But to his credit Tom had calmed down after that and was just getting into a nice rhythm when he witnessed the luckiest hole-in-one anyone could see. Christ if it had been anyone else. He had only just cleared the green writing his name down on the closest to the pin marker after he had struck a beautifully timed 8-iron into the green. The ball finishing little more than two feet away from the hole. No one was beating that he told the rest of his group. Not in this wind.

It was bad enough watching Flannery shunt one into the bunker "under the wind" according to Flannery then watch it skip out and near snap the flag in half before dropping into the hole. Having to watch and hear the celebrations was too much.

But of course, that was in the moment afterwards, in the clubhouse after the round with drinks flowing well then he was just as pleased as everyone else. Delighted. He had bought a celebratory cigar for his old friend. The two were to toast with a glass of whiskey and a smoke on the bridge at the 18th. Stealing the Captaincy. Stealing votes. Offering two of his workforce jobs behind his back. All water under the bridge.

Chapter 9

The Halfway Hut

"If you think it's hard to meet new people, try picking up the wrong golf ball."

24 hours earlier, before any of the drama, the anger, the violence, the murders, could Tom Noonan contemplate playing the wrong bloody ball. The wrong bloody ball. Are you fucking joking. Things were going from bad to worse for Noonan. After picking up somewhat, following a bad start, his game had noticeably deteriorated again over the last couple of holes having witnessed Flannery's hole-in-one at the 7th hole. Correction, having witnessed Flannery's duffed tee shot that somehow inexplicably ploughed through the bunker and out onto the green and into the hole after denting the flagpole. Jaysus. Would they ever hear the end of it. That golf ball needs to be checked. Feck, it practically dug itself out of that feckin' bunker.

Imagine how pleased he was when that Amadan, Jed, Jaysus a village somewhere was missing an idiot, the thick lump, had walked up to the furthest ahead of the two balls lying just yards away from each other on the 9th fairway and set his clubs down looking all pleased with himself. Tom had thought that he might have just outdriven the younger man but you could have thrown a blanket over the two of them so there wasn't much in it.

He was only half paying attention, concentrating on the next shot, remembering the adage that the most important shot in golf is always the next one, and so since he was playing a Callaway Super soft and this seemed to add up with the ball he was preparing to hit, everything appeared in order. He took a practice swing. Looked down at the ball again. Set himself and pulled the trigger. He was pleased with the strike. Whoosh. A flyer that caught a good bounce and looked like it might even creep to the front of the green for an Eagle putt. It got snagged just covering the last few yards before the green. Still, Tom felt good. Pretty sweet. There in two. A chip and a putt. Walk off with a birdie and start putting the round back together. And then that idiot announced that Tom had played his ball.

"Oh, this isn't my ball. You hit mine Tom. Bad luck. Two shot penalty." Bad luck indeed. What a shite. And someone else lucky not to get a club wrapped round their head. What a feckin tool.

The longest hole in golf can be found in South Korea. The honour goes to the 3rd hole at Gunsan Country Club in North Jeolla. The golf resort itself is impressive, with four 18-hole courses and a 9-hole links. The longest hole features on the 3rd at the Country Club, measuring 1,097-yards. It's a par 7. That means getting it in 5 shots counts as a green in regulation for mere mortals. Back at the Chorus Hills Country Club Toms group were playing the 9th hole and it was a long par 5 at 517 yards. Not quite the 1,097 yards but it felt like that to Tom who's desire to continue playing was waning with each hole played, yard walked, shot played. Penalty stroke applied.

So he had played it as a Par 7. Or at least that was the score he had carded thanks to a two-shot penalty. The halfway hut was a welcome sight. At least there were refreshments waiting and he could compose himself. It was customary at the captains' away weekend for the captain to provide an assortment of drinks and snacks for the Society. This started out as some warm sandwiches and tons of beer. Well hold your horses, several years into the ritual and the weekend away had developed, moved on. The old Captains away day had been consigned to history. The days of turning up with your car on the 9th hole and handing out sandwiches from the car boot were long gone. Thankfully.

Keith, that's Captain Keith had excelled himself. There were chilled beers. Not just beers. A choice of brands. You want Morreti, Peroni or Fosters? A couple of token cans of ale for anyone being difficult. There was a bottle of whiskey, little shot glasses and two bottles of port with crackers and cheese resting in the shade alongside some grapes. The Society had come a long way. Christ, there was even a selection of cheese knives to choose from.

Just the ticket. The group in front had already got stuck into the drinks and were hacking away at the cheeses. Hack being the operative word. They were thinking of moving on to the next tee but debating how many beers to take with them. Feck. Tom thought to himself. They have had enough already.

Tom headed straight to the whiskey and calmed his nerves with a quick stiffener. Next up the group got acquainted with the cheese and biscuits. They poured a generous tipple of port and relaxed, pleased to be in the shade at last. Just before Flannery and Co joined them. Tom Noonan applied some more sun cream. You can never be too careful. He had already had skin cancer once and so now applying cream was a ritual. Unfortunately, he felt like he needed to rinse out his eyes. The salty mix of sweat and cream was making his eyes weep again. He took a shot of port. Cheers gents.

He was about to excuse himself when Flannery turned up asking what the hold-up was laughing away to himself. He got a few pats on the back for the hole-in-one before O Keefe told him he was one of the only golfers to shoot an ace and have no idea which direction his ball had gone.

"You know what you remind me of Michael" O'Keefe asked.

"No.. but I'm sure your gonna feckin' tell me" the big oaf replied.

And so O Keefe launches into a joke … "Well now listen to me. There's this young man playing golf with a priest. At a short par 3 the priest asks what are you going to use on this hole son and so the young man says an eight iron, father. How about you… the priest says, I'm going to hit a soft seven iron and pray…. Alright so says the priest and then the young man hits his eight iron and puts the ball on the green. The priest tops his 7 iron and dribbles the ball out a few yards. The young man says I don't know about you father, but in my church when we pray, we keep our head down."

Lots of laughing. Interrupted by Flannery saying "well I hit a good firm 8 iron … not a soft 7 iron under the wind…. You know to let it run in there. And there was no prayer. When you are as good as me you don't need prayer."

Oh yeah right thinks Noonan. Deliberately through the bunker… stop … "the sun shines out of a dog's arse some days" is all Tom Noonan offers before excusing himself to head to the restroom. "Get me a beer someone" he shouts out on his way.

Tom is stood at the urinal urging himself on to have a piss. Come on. What's wrong. Ok relax. The window above him is open. And he can hear O Keefe talking to the two Toms. His Toms. O' Shea and … O' Toole. Noonan is still waiting, twitching his leg to inspire some movement. He can hear everything being said outside. O' Keefe is talking to the guys, his guy, his Toms. He strains his ear to the window to make sure he follows. "Loyalty goes a long way… if you join the team we will have you on the payroll and with an introductory bonus quicker than we can all get wired to the moon …". More laughter. Tom Noonan is finally able to piss.

You feckin maggots Noonan thinks to himself as he returns and the table goes quiet, "OK gents I got one for ye" … Tom Noonan plays along and joins in on the fun.

"Yer man Flannery approaches the priest after church one Sunday and says Father, is it a sin to play golf on Sunday? My son, said the priest, putting his hand on the man's shoulder, I've seen you play golf. It's a sin any day."

More laughter. Even Michael enjoyed that one. A beer and another shot of Port appear. Crackers, Brie and blue cheese. Sound.

Flannery steps up … still walking on air. Nothing is going to take him down a peg or two today. "Ok so one day Jed turns up at this fortune teller and he says to your one, are there golf courses in Heaven? And so, the Fortune Teller replies well I have good news, and I have bad news... Jed says what's the good news? The Fortune Teller tells him the good news is that Heaven's golf courses are beautiful beyond anything you could imagine! And Jed is really happy about that and then asks how could there be any bad news with that? And the Fortune Teller tells him well now the bad news is You have a tee-time at 8:30 tomorrow morning."

Before he gets the final words out Flannery is coughing a lung up and heaving with the effort of his laughter.

Chapter 10

Juggling Einstein's Balls

"To some golfers, the greatest handicap is the ability to add correctly."

Something definitely wasn't adding up in this whole messy affair. Four dead. A party of 21 not 20 across ten, not eleven, rooms. 17 possible suspects at least, more when you looked outside of the Society for a suspect, motive, opportunity. Four bodies across three crime scenes. Four golf balls inserted in the deceased victims. One TikTok Superstar and at least one crazy fucker out there on the loose. Not to mention one major headache for Eagle and his team. Oh and no murder weapon, as of yet. Zero leads. Zero intel, zero witnesses, discounting some noise as recounted by Frank, zero progress you might say. It was early. Very few investigations are solved and put to bed in the first few hours but for Eagle with so little to go on …it was at least imperative that they make some progress. The Commissioner would be on the phone wanting an update within the hour he imagined, actually he was probably on a golf course himself. Hopefully one boasting less crime scene tape and dead bodies than Eagles current location. But that might at least give Eagle a reprieve for a few hours before he had to report in.

On one hand it really was early on in proceedings. And yes, his officers were busy gathering evidence, taking statements, sourcing witnesses, and the forensics team were meticulously working their way through every millimetre of each crime scene, but by this stage someone usually has some semblance of an idea as to what was going on, or rather what went on. It wasn't always that hard to set the scene. Burglary gone wrong. Jealous husband taking revenge, feuding neighbours prank gone wrong, gang land hit …that kind of thing. Whereas four golfers with their heads caved in and some weird ritualistic thing going on with golf balls shoved down or up orifices. Well, that, didn't make sense and certainly didn't fit the profile for any previous investigation Detective Chief Superintendent Nik Eagle had been involved in before or anything one might come across in the manual.

The perfect murder, four of them in one night. Fore! There it was again. Eagle, a huge fan of crime fiction, though this was probably something his colleagues were unaware of, was very much of the opinion that there was no such thing as the perfect murder, only unsolved ones. How to make sense of this chain of events and collection of bodies. How to piece together the end of that night. He was reminded of one of his favourite pieces of writing from Agatha Christie's 'A murder is announced' and he muttered it to himself.

“People with a grudge against the world are aways dangerous. They seem to think life owes them something”. He was much more into his Peter James these days, partly he had to admit because of the sense of familiarity with the locations, but the old classics were what he cut his teeth on when it came to crime and murder mysteries. Come to think of it, Eagle was certain that at least one of her books was set on a golf course. It was something like ‘Murder on the Links’. Anyway, whatever the title it wasn’t her best work.

And so back to the mathematics. Something didn’t add up. But then Eagle didn’t profess to be a mathematician. Like many people he gave up on Maths when the alphabet decided to get involved. Nevertheless, that hadn’t stopped him from creating his own equation in his notebook 4xD +Y= M. Who is M and why the Y? Motive. The only way of finding M in this scenario would be finding a Y, the Motive that was connected to each of the deceased men. Eagle looked at his latest note and his back to front equation. It was time to check in with Jenny and the handbook. Quite what would be ticked off was debatable.

After speaking to Daniel James and convincing him to let them have a copy of the AV files they had gone one better and cajoled him to temporarily hand over his laptop and Mobile. There was something about the way Daniel James simultaneously appeared both super keen to help but also passively reluctant to hand them over that made it more enjoyable to relieve him of them.

"Don't worry we will get them back to you shortly Mr James once we have had a good look at the footage."

"I could just email them over to you" Daniel James helpfully offered.

Eagle pretended not to hear him at first.

"That way I could crack on while these guys are out on the course."

"It's Sunday Daniel … give yourself the day off.. you will barely notice they're gone and you could have captured something from yesterday's antics on the starting line…"

"Tee box." Daniel James interjected.

"Yeah that too."

Daniel James looked like a man debating whether to keep fighting when the battle was lost. Eagle delivered the final blow to put Daniel James out of his misery.

"Your help could be invaluable, an insight into how these guys interact."

Daniel flashed a smile. "Sure. I am not sure it will be any help as it's mainly Gabe vibing. Be careful with them. That's my work and life there."

"They are in safe hands."

Before allowing the guys to head out on the course, something that seemed inexplicably insensitive as far as O' Par was concerned Eagle had quickly caught up with the diamond jumper of Tom Noonan under the pretence of thanking him for his calming words earlier. A sharp man with edges at every turn. A head like a 50 pence piece. Ouch those cheek bones could slice you open. Now there was someone who came across as though he had a grudge against the world. There was not much of him. Not the type of guy who was obviously capable of carrying out 4 murders. But it takes all sorts and Eagle had seen it all in his job. Noonan might look like he might blow away with the wind, but he may have possessed that wiry strength that can take you by surprise. To be continued. Probably just a bit of a twat in Eagle's opinion not killer vibes.

With the Society cleared to go play golf in memory of their fallen brothers in arms, forensics were going to do a quick sweep of each room and Eagle had briefed his officers to turn the rooms upside down once given the all clear to do so by Forensics. They had a few hours, apparently more like 5 hours the way these guys played to find something of use to the investigation, something that might shred some light on who got a bit murdery the night before. Murdery, that was insensitive of him, and he doubted it was a word but if seemed to fit the bill. Someone had done a little more than become a killer. They had lost control and really gone to town.

The clock was ticking …

It was amazing what you could find out in a matter of minutes from the world wide web. Whether or not what you found out was in any way accurate information was another matter altogether. According to the R&A, the governing body of golf, that's another gem Eagle had picked up from scrawling through the internet, there are 38,081 golf courses in 208 countries in the world. Eagle believed that to be a spelling error. Anyone can edit Wikipedia and someone had clearly misspelt counties. According to Eagle most of these courses were situated in England and specifically in or around the two not 208 counties of East and West Sussex. He knew this because, despite never hitting a golf ball in his life, he had visited almost every course in the world by virtue of having the misfortune of being a serial wedding attender. A sort of invited wedding crasher. Invited but never sure if he should be in attendance.

Eagle wasn't really one for attending social occasions but in the 'Force' it seemed that every other week someone was spending money needlessly on their special day. Many of his peers were doing it for a second time, and some like poor old Teddy Divot was on his third. More money than sense Teddy. His latest wife was 25 years his junior. A Pilates instructor. Her legs alone were near as tall as Teddy himself. Fair play to Teddy he had met her at spin class and offered her a lift home in his new Aston Martin and she had fallen in love with him, almost instantly, who would have thought it, Teddy Divot, 25 years her senior with his dodgy knees, toothless smile and Bobby Charlton back combover living his best life and moving from one relationship to the next. She had him out on hikes, on his bike, Pilates classes. Fitness was a full-time job. It was enough to send Teddy to an early grave. Maybe that was the plan. Fitness was overrated as far as Eagle was concerned. But then again Teddy had never been happier.

Maybe there was something to be said for love, if not love, something resembling companionship. Who had time for companionship. Anyway, Eagle had Fin waiting at home for him. A big overweight 10-year-old Labrador. He was company. Eagle was bored of attending weddings and particularly bored of attending weddings at golf courses.

At least he could rely on O' Par. She was already married to the job like him. She didn't seem to mess around with relationships. She was certainly attractive enough to have no shortage of suitors. Listen to me thought Eagle, who would even use the word suitor, but that mouth, that wit, she was lethal. Or Brutal as she would say, although probably in a different context to how he was using it. Invariably they would be one of a small number of their contemporaries who turned up without a plus one. Solidarity. He wondered as she made her way gracefully across the car park at the Chorus Hills Golf and Country club whether she was bored of attending weddings on her own. He wondered whether she was aware of the attention she was getting from the men who had stopped their conversation to watch her glide past.

It was time to consult the Manual. The holy grail. The guidebook ..and get an understanding of where they were. Plus, he knew how much enjoyment O' Par got from ticking off her checklist from the Murder Investigation Model guide.

"Oh, are we doing this here…" O' Par quizzed him as he opened the door for her from the inside.

"Better away from there … we don't just make this shit up Jenny."

"You could have fooled me" O' Par stopped herself as she got in the car and slid into the front passenger seat…. "Holy shite … have you been living in here or something". She moved a number of parking fines from underneath her.

“You should pay some of these you know …”

“It’s fine.

“I know their fines” O’ Par interrupted her boss.

“I save em up and once into double figures I have a pal who works for the council who wipes them off for me.”. O’ Par gave him a look that made him feel like he was a young boy being scolded.

“What! You going to arrest me” Eagle asked defiantly trying to soften his annoyance.

“Well at least it smells better than it looks in here”.

Eagle pointed to the new air freshener. “Found it the other day.”

“Where was it buried underneath an avalanche of feckin parking tickets” O’ Par was squirming in her seat and removed another piece of paper from underneath her. A receipt for a drive-thru McDonalds. Another sign of Eagles meticulous diet.

“It was a present”. She looked at the air freshener.

“Father’s Day present from Nicole.” It read love you to the moon and back. Agh nice. O’ Par knew Eagle had a 15-year-old daughter, but she was living in France with her mum, and they didn’t speak about that part of his life much. Feck it they rarely spoke about anything to do with his personal life.

“Forgot I had it” he reminisced.

Eagle suddenly looked serious. “So” he said, turning the radio down and the air con up.

“We really haven’t got much to go on.”

He read his notes. O’ Par knew she was meant to listen, but they worked best together bouncing off each other and by that she meant with her interrupting him.

“Identify Suspects - well easy enough I suppose but also throw a dart blindfolded at a list of names from the Society.”

“And those not in the society. Your friend Captain Bogey.”

“Or your new boyfriend Daniel James” Eagle laughed.

“Stop he is a kid.”

“Well then everyone from the Receptionist to the greenkeeper.”

“I think we know it’s from within the Group. We will go through the statements and timelines and those who can account for their whereabouts and see who we are left with.”

“We can finally cross off Woosnam” O’ Par chipped in “He will be pleased.”

“Reasons - Now this is a sticking point. 4 guys. All pals. Supposedly well liked.”

“There’s always a reason.”

“Agreed. Let’s find one or several.”

“Bad golf.”

“Bad Jokes.”

“Bad language.”

“Bad men ..maybe they were part of a secret drugs operation…”

“Intelligence Opportunities - Statements, witnesses, acquaint yourself with these asap and let me know what I need to know. I think the team going through the CVTV footage, what limited there is need to get us some idea of movements collaborating or heck they could just find us a homicidal maniac walking around the grounds carrying a weapon covered in blood.”

“Wouldn’t that be nice …”

“ANPR - might as well flag a search for any known wronguns in the area” Eagle added rather weakly for him.

“Witnesses - well we are running on air. Reception spent their time babysitting the lads messing about with the wedding conference equipment and well Frank, we know what Frank heard and that’s it.”

“Someone may well have been a witness without realising it so door to door or rather room to room while we can… anyone still in the vicinity of the crime scenes”.

“Yeah.. let’s get Irons up off his arse and ask him to sort that.”

Eagle glanced down at his notes again. The word “Hole” and Franks pronunciation jumped out at him.

“Postmortem and Forensics” - head trauma x4 is what we have and a case of wait and see for everything else. Likely the same weapon. We have a Footprint in the sand on the 18th and apparently a decent print in blood in room 13.”

“Green will come good. He always does” O’ Par offered and then added “It’s a shame the forensics didn’t pick up anything in the golf equipment or bags.”

“That might have made life too easy for us.”

“Crime Scene assessment. Again, we are going to have to wait for the Forensics to help us on this”.

“Messy, brutal. Not much of a sign of a struggle put up by these fellas but sure they were steaming drunk.”

“Yes, good point, but maybe one of them wasn’t as drunk as they made out and by them, I mean the Group not the deceased.”

“Witness search - ongoing. The team are doing what they can. Let’s skip for now.”

“Victim Enquiries - I have put Balance in charge of a small team. They are speaking with the families and doing the usual searches on finances, phone records etc.”

“She is sound, a wee bit of wagon when out on the town but she’s no eejit that’s for sure.”

“Wagon…Scowled racking his brain for a definition before conceding “in fact don’t tell me.”

“Possible motives” again Eagle consulted his notes. “So far we have shit golf, jealousy of hole-in-one and golf ball envy.” This made O’ Par laugh.

"Agh we are screwed."

"What do you say we arrest that Cockwomble Captain Bogey for being a wanker and get this over and done with."

"Well good debrief I think boss. The manual has told us we are pretty bad at our jobs."

"Come on let's head back to the station. You have some TiK Tok videos to watch… and speak for yourself. I am great at my job. The manual is useful but people.. understanding and watching people that is more important."

He screeched out of the car park and then realised he had the world's longest driveway to navigate again and speed bumps lined up like dominoes and felt immediately deflated. Still, he could always look forward to tea and biscuits back at the station.

"Did you know that Einstein hated golf" Eagle broke the silence.

"Are you comparing yourself to Einstein you big Dope."

"No but so there is a story"…

"Christ have you been on the internet again…"

“No well yes but Einstein is convinced to try his hand at golf.. just a lesson while visiting some university or other...and the pro is desperate to help this genius…so he keeps issuing further instructions every time Einstein fails to hit the ball” …

“Agh well you can’t be good at everything.”

“The pro starts shouting out too many instructions and irritates Einstein and he eventually loses his cool”.

“He loses his rag, Einstein.”

“Something like that anyway don’t interrupt finally he asks the pro for a handful of balls, and he throws them all up at the pro shouting catch and the pro fails to catch any of them. The point he is trying to make is that if he throws one ball the pro catches it but 4 at the same time, he catches nothing… so you know one point at a time... one ball at a time.”

“Bollix. Never happened trust me.”

Eagle couldn’t help but laugh. “So cynical. The point .. and there is a point Jenny … is we are juggling too many balls here… AND there is only one that matters, Michael Flannery. The others are collateral damage… however insensitive and dismissive that seems right now. The staging of the body… the brutality… the motive for him leads to the killer of all 4. We don’t need to catch all 4 balls .. we just need to catch one.”

"Agh Jaysus are we back onto these feckin balls…turns out you're the same as every other man back at the station with the obsession with your balls."

"Put your seat belt on … why do I put up with you…"

"If I could see the belt through the feckin tickets I would."

She always has to have the last word. Then it happens his phone flashes and a call is incoming from the Commissioner, no doubt checking in from the course himself …

Fuck thought Eagle.

"Shouldn't you take that one Sir."

"No Jenny we should almost certainly not take that one".

"What's all this we."

Chapter 11

Two Left Feet

"Golf is a compromise between what your ego wants you to do, what experience tells you to do, and what your nerves let you do."

Experience told Jenny O' Par that if you hadn't come across the evidence you were after you simply hadn't looked in the right places.

Back at HQ armed with a coffee and a pack of rip-off jammy dodger biscuits, O' Par was going to review the footage from Daniel James. Buy cheap pay twice, was Eagles motto on the copycat products but biscuits were biscuits. O' Par's focus was the footage taken on the 1st tee from the previous day. This would have included the material used to produce the two reels she had already watched with Eagle. The latest reels to go live on Triple Gs TikTok and well whatever else he had filmed. The society had all been waiting around the 1st so perhaps they also featured in the peripheries. Of course, it might be an absolute dead end so she might not even get through the biscuits.

Hydration doesn't take a day off. Another of Eagles pearls of wisdom, O' Par realised she was gasping and downed a bottle of water while her coffee cooled down. The tech team had logged her into Daniel James laptop and mobile so she had full access and wouldn't be locked out and the 'Geek' aka Graham Pratt, he preferred the name Geek, well wouldn't you if you were called Graham Pratt, had copied the audio-visual files across already. She was ready to go.

Earlier she had spoken to the captain of the Birchgrove Irish Golf Society, a man called Keith, a man, more like walking dead earlier that morning. In truth the guy was probably incapable of organising a piss up in brewery, so she assumed he was captain in name only he had woken up with eyes like piss holes in the snow. Keith was not an organiser. Jenny O' Par knew that from the outset. Christ the guy had woken up absolutely hanging or he had woken up still bollocksed according to Jenny O' Pars vocabulary. Keith had opened his eyes that morning and the first thing he saw was the cardboard cutout bride from the wedding conference that he had taken to bed with him the previous night. It had taken him a few moments to differentiate cardboard from real life. No Keith had had a lot of help in putting this get-together, well together at all.

She had quickly come to the conclusion that the two guys who seemed to have some idea of what was going on were the same ones who had the misfortune of informing the family left behind of their loved one's departure from this world. Jonny Rosewait and Joseph Mcilroy, no relation unfortunately to Rory. Her father would have loved that. Rory McIlroy was her father's favourite player and Joseph, must have anticipated the question so pointed out from the start he was no relation.

These two gentlemen had seemed genuinely shocked and unsettled by what had happened and had given her a quick rundown on the Society, its pecking order and what happens at these events, other than copious amounts of drinking. Jaysus, it really is like herding cats with these feckers .... We do everything but wipe their arses .... And they still complain.

There is always an expectation from some society members, and this is true of those that turn up to regular club competitions too that everything has been arranged purely for their enjoyment, it really is turn up and play.

They turn up … expect to be fed and watered and on a weekend like this load up on a few pints before a ball is hit which makes them even less likely to pay attention to any instruction. The trick is to have one guy in each group who is less Bollocksed than the others and can remember his name at the end of the round. Always have someone sensible out front to carry the closest to the pin and longest drive markers out there, if you haven't been organised enough to get the pro shop to put these out for you. The idea was to mix up playing groups, so they were random over the couple of rounds. The ethos was to get to know and enjoy everyone's company. Unfortunately, in Michael's Group he had made a heavy pitch to influence his playing fourball. Jonny had given in to shut him up and get some peace. O' Par couldn't help but think this had been a significant decision and the repercussions more so. Death being a serious repercussion.

Before settling down to tune in to Daniel James footage she checked in at the course and it looked like slowly they were getting an idea of who was with who and when for the evening and night before. But throughout it all the narrative was the same. These guys basically liked each other and enjoyed each other's company. There was no one capable of murder, correction, we are all capable, there was no one who would want to take another life or have reason to do so.

The laptop came to life and before it was paused Daniel James had been playing a song she liked. 'Just Say Yes' the band escaped her but it was an Irish band she was sure of that. She would often squabble over control of the airwaves with Eagle, and he would simply tell her she hadn't a clue what music was. She could hear his voice echo inside her head… "Back in my day we knew what real music was"… Needless to say, they rarely agreed on a playlist. Or for that matter even a song.

She turned off his music on the laptop and set about clicking on the videos. The footage in the folder dated and marked live was the camera on Gabe and it was marked 'Hoodie Promo' but there was a second folder marked 'alright on the night' a mobile link up.

O' Par instinctively clicked on the folder marked 'alright on the night' and pressed play. The clip marked test was full on Blair Witch product material and made her dizzy. Camera shaking around until it was focused in on the first tee and the impressive camera that was set up already in situ to capture Gabe's routine. O' Par was watching Mobile phone footage recording the shoot. After the initial grainy wobbling it was good quality. The 'it will be alright on the night' folder was in many ways a voyeuristic watch, a kind of the -making-of type scenario. Good idea O' Par thought. A different perspective.

So next up, it cut to Daniel James who could be seen setting up the main camera on the first tee and Gabe was running through some moves, it was hot, and he was wearing a hoodie and some heavy jewellery. Daniel was there in his own hoodie trying to stay largely out of shot.

They ran through a couple of routines, Gabe looking a little awkward like he couldn't really remember what he was meant to be doing and Daniel patiently coaxing him and telling him he was doing great, "Remember the hips, the swagger, the arms. Own it Gabe. You are a superstar dude. Millions of people waiting to see this."

The continuous shot suddenly becomes pretty useless, at least from a visual standpoint as some men walk past and put their clubs down obscuring the view. It's obviously guys from the Society strapping themselves in to see what is going on. Here to support their resident social media superstar O' Par concludes.

She is wrong. Not much support on show. They are out of sight, but very much in earshot … the sound control is surprisingly faultless.

"Your man looks like a feckin eejit doesn't he dancing around like a Jack in a box …."

"I will tell you what he looks like. He looks like he has a swarm of wasps trapped in his pants."

"I have seen a hot air balloon turn quicker."

"Well, I could probably dance better than that with a feckin flagpole up me hole …"

“Wait he might well have a pole up his arse.”

“Or some love eggs … Jaysus sure aren’t Titleist doing them now … they think of everything ….”

“A bad dancer always has trouble with his balls” (laughter and a piggy snort).

“Jaysus … what’s he doing there … he looks like he is looking for his keys.”

“Agh look the only dancing he should do is pole dancing .. holding onto the safety pole in the bathtub.”

“He has two left feet but one must be right wouldn’t u think.”

Jenny O’ Par doesn’t want to watch anymore, or rather listen but she can’t draw herself away. The comments are endless.

“Well now there are only two things stopping him from being a good dancer.. his feet.”

More laughter. More piggy snorting.

“Well for the love of God he is dancing like a stripper whose rent is due tomorrow… Christ.”

Lots of laughter…

“Can you imagine if we filmed this shite… well you could stick your TikTok …”

“Oh You are filming… you can send that into You’ve been framed.”

Laughter followed by silence. Muffled sounds. Someone seems to point to the phone camera. A finger suddenly appears.

“Right gents team Flannery is up soon .. grab a couple of beers and saddle up once this eeejit has been voted off the dance floor.”

“It’s a no from me.”

Sniggering and more laughter … they move aside and Gabe is taking off his hoodie and getting a high five from Daniel James… good work.

There is a round of applause from the rest of the group gathering around.

They say opportunity dances with those already on the dance floor … O' Par was watching Gabe do his thing in the distance to Commentary that didn't reflect the end result … perhaps a testimony to Daniel James editing skills … but nevertheless the comments, the critique from Gabe's peers, his friends, seemed really harsh! Was it just jest. Jealousy. They each went up and congratulated Gabe … after so perhaps it was just bravado.

Daniel had been reluctant to hand over the footage … probably just trying to protect Gabe from the humiliation of hearing that shit from his so-called friends. Sweet lad she thought to herself. Cute too. But young. Too young.

O' Par tried to take in what she had just seen, or rather heard. So she played it again and it was even harder to hear.

You have to dance as if there were no one watching you, love as though you have never been hurt, sing as if there is no one listening to you, and live as if this were heaven on earth. Jaysus not with these eejits looking on.

As much as she wanted to laugh off the banter. It was reminiscent of a pack mentality. Triple G was the target. Maybe something was said. O' Par wanted to catch up with Daniel James and find out if Triple G had seen this footage. He might well be very upset.

Right good idea Eagle agreed after being brought up to speed. "But while your at it… what did Daniel James think of the crap he had recorded. He seems pretty fond of Gabe." Eagle had watched, sorry again heard, what O' Par did and agreed it was tough. Banter but perhaps with a tinge of vitriol.

"Oh there is something else"…

"Go on" Eagle perked up.

"It carries on. There is something else you need to see."

Fast forward to a scene on the tee box. Flannery has put his bag down and is talking to Tom Noonan who places his ball down on a tee. He looks a little distracted. Practice swing practice swing and then whoosh.

Cue laughter, jumping around, and Flannery shouting "do the rest of ye want to play off the men's tee."

Noonan looks disgusted. Something else is said that is a bit muffled. Eagle makes out the words wife and play. And then Noonan looks up at one of the other men and waves his club at him and can be heard saying “You won’t be laughing with this wrapped around your head.”

Wow. A game changer. A threat to hit one of the men who got their skulls crushed. A threat to wrap a club around his head.

Chapter 12

Lightning strikes twice

"Golf is a good walk spoiled."

Walking down the 3rd hole at Chorus Hills, Tom Noonan felt like a new man. Refreshed. The anger he felt the previous night had gone. He was in a reflective mood. Life is not a dress rehearsal. You have to grab each opportunity with both hands. Death brings that home. Especially death close to home. Whatever happened to Flannery and the three Toms, well that was their business. Michael Flannery, God love his soul may he rest in peace, had always mixed with unsavoury types and done favours through the books on jobs against Noonan's wishes. Anything for a quick buck. And Flannery had made a lot of money. Tom hadn't done so bad himself. He was about to do a lot better. He realised that there was a whole lot of people with jobs and orders with Flannery's cowboy outfit who would now be turning to Tom Noonan and TN Cement to pick up the pieces and finish the job. Well, that's what you get when you fly by the seat of your pants and go with the cheapest option. But cheap pay twice.

Noonan wouldn't be surprised one bit if the police assumed he had been bumped off by one of the many unsavoury characters he did business with. That would put him in the clear. Hopefully someone was already looking into his business affairs. He regretted saying some of the things he said the previous day but sad as it was that Flannery had passed away, he probably had it coming. The man was a waking heart attack. I mean, how long did he actually have left anyway, even if he hadn't pissed of some crime syndicate asking to help launder money or whatever it was this time that he had got himself into. Not just himself. This time he had dragged that little monkey sidekick O'Keefe into it and his Toms, the little turncoats, well how did that end up for them. Again, as sad as it was and he had enjoyed many good times with them, they had outstayed their welcome.

We had some good times buddy he thought to himself but Michael your time had come. Who had you pissed off now. Tom Noonan looked up at what was in front of him. 145 yards to the green. Wind behind. It was a firm 8 iron for him so he looked inside his bag and selected his club. Practice swing. Step back. Align himself with the V shape between the trees lying behind the green. The wind from the left, just slightly. Another practice swing. Feeling slightly unbalanced, Tom Noonan addresses the ball and then stops. His playing partners look up at him. Tom lifts up his club and immediately realises this isn't his club. He takes a close look. It's an 8-iron, just not his. A Ping G430 steel shaft, heavier than Tom's own clubs. He has seen this bloody club in his nightmares. Flannery's club. Flannery's 8 iron. The hole-in-one club that he brought down to dinner sat next to him. The same club that spent the evening with him. The same club that got bought a drink for every drink a very drunk and boisterous Michael Flannery drank. The very same damned club that got toasted more times than a bride at a wedding.

What the fuck he thinks to himself. How has this ended up in my bag. He places the club back into his bag and stands over his clubs pondering which club to use, somewhat worried that his own 8-iron has been swapped out. No there it is. One moment he calls out. Jed, how the heck has he ended up playing with that cretin again, Jed is getting restless and wants to play his shot. Tom had already rebuked him for playing out of turn earlier on the 1st hole. Nothing like a friendly game. "Ready golf…ready golf Tom" Jed had retorted pointing animatedly at his watch indicating that he thought Tom was taking too long to play his shot. Noonan finds his own 8-iron and plays his shot. Perhaps rushing a bit. It's pin high but drifts a little right. Didn't aim at the V between the trees behind the green. Flustered. He casts Jed a death stare for rushing him. The big lump is oblivious. Noonan tries to forget that Flannery's 8-iron is resting in his bag, but it is playing on his mind. Why? Why is it in his bag and when and how did it get there.

Day 2 was a much more subdued affair. That tends to happen around death. Probably more so around murder. Brutal, frenzied ones at that. One man was doing his best to put the events of the previous day behind him, and not to mention the morning at that. How dare she interrupt his practice on the range and remove him like that. He had only hit 79 of his 100 balls and was barely into his warm-up drill. When Jed Evans had the bit between his teeth he was like a dog with a bone. He wouldn't give up. His razor like focus had been reignited now he was in contention. With 4 members not playing, albeit because they were dead Jed was pretty sure he just needed to stay composed to see it home. Win the day. Then the next thing he knew, just as he was getting the big gun out, his driver for the last push, the little mouthy detective was more or less asking him what the fuck he was doing and dragging him off the range. She had even asked him if he was away with the fairies. No just practicing was his response.

As far as Jed was concerned a golfer has to train his swing on the practice tee, then trust it on the course. You can't just rock up and expect to smash your first drive down the middle of the fairway. So many of his contemporaries turned up, had a cup of tea and hit 4 or 5 token putts on the putting green. Some more adventurous might hit a couple of balls in the net. What a hopeless bunch. No Jed liked to be at the course at least 90 minutes before tee off. Get in a solid 45-minute practice and then stop for a pork based breakfast bap and then hit the putting green. It was Gary Player who said the harder you practice the luckier you get.

To win the weekend he might just need a little bit of luck. His nearest rival Tom was playing well, but slowly, too slow for Jed. If his calculations were correct Jed had started his day two shots ahead of Noonan and the two were equal through three holes thus far. But the slow play. It was getting to him. Jed had already used his favourite line on the first hole while Tom Noonan had pondered over a shot from the fringe carrying two clubs putter and wedge. “Come on Tom I started the round clean shaven.”

Tom wasn’t amused and had glared at him in a way that had made Jed shut up. That lasted a hole. On the second Green when Tom was faced with a putt that was a bit of a James Joyce, he had walked around the hole to view his putt from every possible angle Jed had boldly declared “Tom you know why you keep leaving your putts short? Because the grass grows between the time you line it up and finally putt it".

Tom wasn’t amused and had told Jed he had grass growing between his ears. But then after the third or was it fourth hole Tom had become distracted and keen to end the round. Maybe it was because after watching Tom push his approach on the third a little right Jed had cashed in the luck; he felt his practice deserved. He hit a high wedge into the green and it popped up high off the sprinkler and landed in the hole. Boom. Slam dunk. Tom was disgusted. Jed was ecstatic.

Things went from bad to worse for Tom Noonan on the 4th tee. A nice, picturesque par 3 leading towards the valley. Elevated tee. Large green protected by several bunkers either side and in front of the green and with a back board slope at the back sending everything long back towards the hole. After Jed's Eagle at 3 he steps up to the tee full of confidence and drills a 9 iron into the bank, watching, twisting his body from side to side as the ball lands softly and slowly trundles back towards the green picking up pace, edging ever closer to the pin. Jed can barely control himself as he tries to steer the ball to the hole using the power of his contorted body. A hole-in-one. His first ever hole-in-one. Back-to-back eagles. A bloody hole-in-one. "Yes!!! Yesssssssssss" he cried out thumping his chest wandering over to every corner of the tee box like he is a WWF wrestler playing up to the crowd. His playing partners, Brendan, Frank and Tom, all congratulate him looking at each other in astonishment, while thinking back 24 hours and what happened in the aftermath of Flannery's hole-in-one. Sit down you feckin Amadan is what Tom is thinking. Jed is oblivious. He has fallen to his knees and is kissing the club like he has just scored the winning goal in a World Cup final and is kissing the badge in front of his adoring fans.

It takes a few minutes for Jed to calm down. When he does Tom steps up to tee off. He pulls out his 8-iron, except it's not his, again the wrong 8 iron appears in his hand. He turns it over inspecting it closer. He knows it is not his, that has already been established but there is something odd about it. He inspects it. There are dark streaks in the grooves, the heel of the club also has Burgundy patched in the indents. Lumpy gristle clinging to the contours of the branded insignia. This is Flannery's hole-in-one club, and someone has put it in his bag. Tom wants to vomit. Is it blood. What are the little lumps?

Chapter 13

Look Out Ahead

"I hit two good balls on the course today. I stepped on a rake."

Eagle was about to get a stiff kick in the balls in the form of an unwanted call from the commissioner.

Fore! It must be the most often repeated muttering on the course at least, amongst those that could be repeated. Others include using one's own name in disgust immediately after striking the ball. Obviously, any 4-letter profanity will invariably trump all else but when it comes to those terms willingly spoken aloud on the course, FORE! Must win out. Fore, widely known as the golfers' way to warn others on the course of impending danger, that danger coming in the form of a little white dimpled ball flying through the air usually at speed. Fore is a shortened version of an old Scottish warning "afore" which basically meant "look out ahead". Of course, its origins were Scottish or more than likely Scottish. We are dealing with golf after all. Consider this, the people who gave us golf and called it a game are the same people who gave us the bag pipes and called it music. They, being the Scottish. Or perhaps that is a myth, it has been suggested that the true origins of the game of golf can actually be traced back to a game in China involving hitting rocks with sticks.

Eagle was all for warnings. It helped to be forewarned especially at a time when the force and policing in general was under scrutiny from every angle. He wasn't one for surprises. Not for all the tea in China. He liked to be thoroughly informed with the facts before he went into any debrief and he most certainly didn't enjoy speaking with the Commissioner under any circumstance where the Commissioner might know something he didn't. This is precisely why he was fuming after receiving a call from the Commissioner informing him that apparently, they had their man. That was the news from Chorus Hills Golf and Country Club. The news that had somehow bypassed Eagle. The call itself had interrupted an interesting development and O' Par was in the middle of updating her boss when the interruption came.

One of the Statements taken earlier that day had suggested that there was more than a hint of animosity between Tom Noonan and the fourball made up of Michael Flannery, Tom O'Keefe, Tom O' Shea and Tom O' Toole. That being the fourball, the fourball made up of the four victims. The four men who now lay dead, on their way to the Mortuary. This news came courtesy of Seamus, who was rooming with Frank, these two were a veritable plethora of information, they may as well be on the payroll. O' Par had learned that Michael Flannery had offered O' Shea and O' Toole, currently, or at least at time of their untimely deaths employed by Tom Noonan, the chance to join Flannery's outfit. Together with O'Keefe, he had offered them jobs with more money and a whole load of incentives to jump ship. And that wasn't all, but before O' Par could continue, Eagles phone was buzzing across the desk.

Eagle answered taking in a deep breath. "Eagle, I don't have long, apparently you have your man, no confession yet but Rupert Bogey, good man I believe you bumped into him, wasn't a fan of yours to be honest but that's understandable on first impression, takes a bit of time doesn't it. anyway, well he told me that your officers had taken someone away … good job… let's tidy up the course and get out of there… I am playing there on Tuesday last thing I want is a bunker out of action, especially if some bugger is laying in there with his backside on display."

"Well actually Sir…" before Eagle could attempt to play down whatever as yet unknown development had taken place, the Commissioner was busy replying to someone on the other end.. "make it a double." Eagle didn't for a second think that retort was for him but with one final parting shot "Eagle, keep me informed and I mean of every damn thing", the Commissioner had ended the call leaving Eagle contemplating whether he was angry that he didn't get a chance to temper expectations or pleased that he had dodged a bullet by not having to admit he was out of the loop of this latest development.

"Somebody needs to tell me what the fuck is going on and then explain why the fucking Commissioner knows something about our case that I don't."

"Agh would you relax. You'll give yourself a heart attack."

"Get me Floggy on the line." Detective Inspector Stuart Flog was a young detective in Eagles team. Very capable. Dry sense of humour. Took himself perhaps a little too seriously. He was meant to be coordinating things at the course until Eagle and O' Par returned.

Poor Floggy was about to get an earful but was saved just in time. A plump red-faced desk sergeant entered the room after a hefty knock on the door to deliver a message.

"Sorry to trouble you Sir, DI Floggy has been trying to get hold of you. Left a message to ask that you get back to the course. There has been a development."

Eagle attempted to calm himself down by concentrating on the Desk Sergeants shiny head and its reflective qualities. He then turned his attention to a plate of biscuits, before grabbing one and nodding at O' Par. "Well come on then, let's get going. Get Floggy on the phone" …. he then added a "please" remembering that he was talking to O' Par and it might be in his best interests to be polite.

They had planned to return to the course anyway but figured they had another 30 minutes or so to see what progress they could make on the statements and work out what they might need to discuss with Triple G and Yer man Angry Tom as newly christened by O' Par. They were unsure whether Gabe would have had an opportunity to view or rather hear the footage mocking his performance, perhaps Daniel James could shed light on that particular issue. The threat from Tom Noonan on the 1st tee had been real and given the events that followed, while it might well have been laughed off as said in jest, the statements indicating at least a sprinkling of animosity suggested Noonan really did need questioning.

O' Par and Eagle set off on their way back to the Chorus Hills Golf and Country Club. The weather had changed in the time they had spent back at the Station. Blue sky had been painted over with a dull grey and there were dark clouds overseeing proceedings ominously.

"That's a dirty looking sky" O' Par declared as she worked Bluetooth on the car and Stuart Flog's name flashed up on a screen on the dashboard.

“Boss” came a cheery greeting from DI Stuart Flog.

“Sorry to interrupt your nap Floggy” Eagle was keen to let the young detective know that not answering within the first 3 rings was a crime. DI Flog was smart enough to realise the response from his boss was somewhat less cheery.

“Bit manic down here all of a sudden boss. Did you get my message.”

“I did. We are on our way back. I have O’ Par with me.”

“Jen”…

“Stuey” she replied by way of acknowledgement. Eagle hadn’t heard him called Stuey before and wondered how well these two knew each other.

“Well come on what’s the craic.”

“She means what have you got for us Stuey.” Eagle accentuated the last word.

Caught off guard DI Flog cleared his throat before delivering his news. “We got one of the golfers from the Society waiting to speak to us… well you once you are here but he found an extra club in his bag. Came and found us after they finished their round.”

An extra club in his bag. Full circle back to this Woosnam character and extra clubs in the bag. “Right what am I meant to do disqualify him or something…” Eagle was becoming impatient but DI Flog was quick to get to the point.

“Well, the club appears to have belonged to one of the deceased. This guy recognised it. And well, it may have traces of blood and other matter on it.”

O’ Par shot Eagle a look. A weapon. A murder weapon. At last.

“Any Forensics still on scene.”

“Irons stopped one of Green’s team in the car park just before they left.”

“Great get it examined straight away. Be there in twenty minutes” Eagle couldn’t hide the fact that a minuscule amount of enthusiasm had jolted him into life.

O’ Par jumped in “Stu”.. not Stuey this time, “who have you got with you?

“The guy who found the club in his bag is a Tom Noonan… he is a bit shaken. Very concerned as to how the club got in his bag and the gunk on the club.”

Again, another look between the two in the car. Surely too easy. Motive and a weapon dropping into their laps. DI Flog wasn’t finished.

"It's an 8-iron". This meant nothing to Eagle.

DI Flog offered up one more piece of information that Noonan had given him. "It belonged to Michael Flannery. The guy in the bunker."

"Agh the hole-in-one club" O' Par chipped in.

"That's the one Jenny."

"Floggy, can you explain to me why the Commissioner thinks we are about to arrest someone" Eagle didn't attempt to hide his irritation.

"Like I said Sir it's a bit manic down here and we have had this pain in the arse wanting to talk to us about the course. Following me around like a shadow. He was in reception when Noonan came to us with the club" …. Eagle unleashed an inaudible grunt which may have masked a profanity. "I had Noonan escorted away into one of the rooms so we could talk in peace."

"That Gobshite Bogey" O' Par couldn't help blurt out.

"Yeah, that's him. Knows the Commissioner and has told us all a thousand times. Decided that we had arrested someone. I told him to mind his bloody business and make himself scarce."

"Well that's you off the Commissioners Christmas Card list too. Feel free to arrest him and Floggy, keep him away from wherever Noonan is. Let's try and keep this to ourselves."

As the call ended the rain that was threatening as the sky grew darker suddenly came pounding down. Eagle flicked the window wipers on and one of them was squeaking keeping perfect time.

"Jaysus does anything work in this shit heap" O' Par played with the controls in an attempt to put the heater on. It had suddenly turned cold. But the good news was the case was heating up.

"Tom Noonan" Eagle offered and breathed out a deep blast of air. "If we have a weapon, a golf club, and Noonan was the maniac wielding it like an axe the previous night …why on earth would he keep the club in his bag and then come and give it in".

"Maybe he is making it look like he is being framed."

"Not buying that."

"I bet ya he uses the line if I was a murderer why would I leave the murder weapon yadda yadda yadda … you know the rest."

"That's if the club is a weapon."

"Look sure we needed to speak to him anyway. Remember angry Tom was already a person of interest before this."

Eagle had to agree. It would make things nice and tidy but also the extra club in the bag thing. No this didn't sit right.

“Look out” and with that Eagle pressed down hard on the brakes as a deer jumped out across the road ahead of them and disappeared into a gap that didn’t exist in the hedge.

“Well the Feckin brakes work at Least.”

Eagle turned on the radio and immediately turned it off again.

“I like that song” O’ Par protested.

Eagle shook his head. “The youth of today.”

“Would you cop on I’m only ten years younger than you.”

“I am old before my time.”

“Well that’s true” … and something reminded O’ Par she hadn’t finished updating her boss on the Statement from Seamus Conlon.

“So, Yer man Flannery hadn’t just offered the Toms jobs they were conditional on their support for his proposal for Captaincy.”

“Which means what” Eagle asked.

“Well according to Seamus, there were two candidates for Captaincy this year. Tom Noonan and now Michael Flannery. Tom was meant to be unopposed but went from a cert to just nudging it on probable votes.”

Eagle pretends to yawn.

“Your such an Eeejit. If his Toms x 2 defected over to Flannery, then Flannery would be Captain.”

“Ok Jenny if, if Noonan even knew about this. Why would he actually give two fucks. Are you telling me being captain of a whackfuck club was so important that he might go all frenzied murderer.”

“No more than he might over some feckin golf balls” O’ Par laughed.

“It’s all highly improbable Jenny. Something tells me we are being led on a wild goose chase.”

“That’s my favourite kind of goose chase” Jenny O’ Par switched the radio back on and much to her surprise Eagle didn’t object. Murder on the Dance floor was playing and she wondered whether he was trying to suppress singing the same version that was running through her head. He didn’t disappoint “It’s murder on the golf course….” Eagle bellowed out. He was blessed with volume. It came naturally to him but he was no singer.

Eagle screeched the car into the extended Driveway leading to the Chorus Hills Golf and Country Club. “This bastard driveway and speed bumps are enough to make you want to kill.”

“I’d just be happy if this rust bucket is still in one piece by the time we make the car park.”

Chapter 14

A murder is announced

"There's no such thing as bad weather, only inappropriate clothing".

He just needed to weather the storm but kept remembering how the detectives had spoken to him. Was he being paranoid or were they suspicious of him. Perhaps detectives were all just naturally suspicious of everything. They had been polite enough and engaging almost but the questions were relentless. The guy, Eagle was a bit gruff round the edges but had lightened up. Perhaps a bit rude at times about what he did for a living but social media and being an influencer wasn't for everyone. Being Triple G was a full-time job. The young female detective, well she had friendly eyes, which helped put him at ease but equally she seemed a little more on the ball than the older detective. She looked like she didn't miss a trick and you could almost see her mind ticking over as her eyes darted across the room always taking in everything. He almost always felt on edge after filming and then there was the golf itself. The last thing he needed especially after a long night was a grilling on number of followers, and how the whole thing worked. The last 24 hours had aged him. He felt sapped of energy.

He was not sure he could hold up if there was much more to come in the way of questioning. Hopefully they had been thrown off the scent. Why so bloody suspicious. Even if he had killed 4 people the previous evening. It's not as though he set out to do that. Once he had the club in hand and that oaf Flannery had refused to hand over his phone. Well, he had seen red. And he can't say it didn't feel good bringing that club down on his head. That didn't make him a killer. Well except it did. Obviously, that is exactly what made him, a killer. He was not a premeditated murderer. The other three just sort of followed suit. At any time, they could have changed their respective fates by being less obstinate, less obtrusive, less macho, more complicit. He was no murderer after all. Just out to preserve what he had built.

Earlier in the evening Flannery had become unbearable. He could hear him getting louder increasing the volume of his God-awful laugh with each drink. There he was toasting his club. Laughing and joking as though he had just won the Open Championship. Telling everyone about his hole-in-one and the footage from the 1st tee. "No I am telling ye. We will be sending that into you've been framed." If it wasn't that he was telling everyone how he thought he would make the perfect Tik Tok star.

"8 million …8 million is that all. I would be expecting at least 80 million I tell ya."

When Michael Flannery finally paused for breath, he wondered outside taking his club and cigar with him. The cigar had been provided by Tom Noonan. The two of them were gonna bury their differences over a smoke. Like old times. He couldn't find Noonan and so headed out alone.

Look at that fool. Flannery was stood cigar in one hand and golf club in the other. Flannery was stood on the bridge like some peacock flapping his wings, so he approached him quietly not wishing to startle him, well until he did. "Jaysus what the feck are you doing out here. You scared the life out of me".

Watching Flannery as he refused to hand his phone over angered him.

"I suggest you feck off out of it. I don't have the footage. It wasn't me filming that God awful shite."

Flannery turned his back on him, rested his club against the bridge handrail and puffing on in his cigar, dropped his trousers. "I need a pish and well you can kiss my arse." And with that Michael Flannery had turned his back on him and ended the conversation while pissing into the moat from the bridge.

How dare you turn your back on me. He couldn't help it. He picked up the club and wallop. He struck Flannery so hard down on the head he collapsed. His legs buckled. He managed to catch him otherwise he might have even ended up in the moat. A quick look around. It was all quiet out here. He dragged him, no easy task, with Flannery's trousers falling down lower and lower around his ankles with each movement. He dragged him round to the deep bunker behind the green. Careful not to disturb the green and pushed him face down into the bunker. The great oaf had made one last dive falling into the sand much like he fell into bed most nights.

In the movies these things tend to take time. Several blows. Protagonists fight it out administering blow after blow until one finally succumbs to a killer blow. In real life, that wasn't how things happened. The blow to the back of the head had made a mess of Flannery's skull chipping away at a piece of bone and denting the back of his head out of shape. He was pleased to get rid of him. Put some distance between them. He took a step back and was able to survey what he had done. The injury wasn't pleasant to look at. But he didn't feel remorse.

Triple G wasn't going to go down without a fight. He wasn't going to be humiliated by so called friends. He picked up two items from the ground outside of the bunker that had fallen. Two sleeves of balls. He had his gloves on. Light touch personalised gloves. He could still use his phone. They were a gift from the agency to mark 1 million followers. One of many. He managed to get hold of Flannery's phone and frantically searched for photos and videos. Nothing. Oh! wait hang on. Photo after photo of a smiling Michael Flannery with golf ball held aloft and club held aloft. It was cold all of a sudden. The temperature had dropped. He could scc his brcath. There was plenty of noise coming from the bar. Singing and laughter the night was still young for some. It was only 75 yards away. Satisfied that the footage he was after wasn't there on Flannery's phone, He threw the phone into the moat where seconds ago Flannery had been taking a leak. Rest in peace. And then he remembered Flannery's words.

"I could dance better with a flagpole up my hole."

And then it happened. He removed a ball from the sleeve of an unopened pack of Pro V1s and shoved a ball up Flannery's backside. He then went and retrieved the flag from the 18th hole and brought it over to where Flannery lay, trousers round his ankles, bare bottom on display in the pitch black. Let's see how you dance now he said to himself planting the flag violently in its new hole.

Where next? The most likely person to have filmed the footage for his boss was Tom O Keefe. TK. I guess it was a case of talking to the monkey rather than the organ grinder for a change. And so he found the fire escape stairs that he had located earlier in the day by mistake. And made his way up to the 2nd floor armed with Flannery's key card. He made his way into the room trying to catch his breath and compose himself. Expecting to find TK in bed a little worse for where he was surprised to find that TK was nowhere to be found despite apparently heading to bed some time ago.

What to do. In some ways he was relieved. Was he going to attack him in bed. Confront him? Or just try and steal his phone? Before he can decide on his next move he was kickstarted into action by a noise in the corridor immediately outside. Where to hide, oh god where to hide. The bed. He dropped to the floor and scrambled in under the bed. His body was aching. Some of those dance routines made muscles he didn't know he had ache. He wasn't as young as he once was.

What followed surprised him. It also got him thinking. He had after all just killed someone. Unless that was, he had imagined Flannery's crushed skull.

TK had been followed into the room by someone. Someone angry. It was Tom Noonan. They exchanged a series of angry words. Loyalty. Snakes. Revenge. It didn't last long but Noonan departed after promising to shove a golf club up TK's hole and adding something about bollocks and eyeballs.

Something was digging into his sides. It was the golf balls in his pockets. To make matters worse he was half laying on a golf club. Flannery's 8-iron.

After Noonan had stormed off to find Flannery. Good luck with that. TK went into the bathroom and was certainly surprised to see him. "What are you doing here".

He told him straight up. He needed his phone.

"Would ye just feck off to hell".

Stood there with a pocket full of golf balls and Flannery's 8-iron he instinctively pointed to the door as if he was pointing something out and when TK turned his back to look at the door he brought the club down with as much force as he could muster.

Outside, doors are opening and shutting. TK looks like he simply might just be sleeping. Taking some time out. There is however an ever-expanding pool of blood on the floor. Wiping the club on a golf towel hanging down from a set of clubs thrown down in front of the TV, he again removes the opened pack of golf balls and removes another ball leaving one in the sleeve. You had a big mouth on you. Well, the truth can be hard to swallow and finds a home for another golf ball.

He feels a little bit of nausea. It's time for fresh air. He runs to the fire escape with TKs phone in his hand and golf club in the other, towel shoved in his pocket. TKs phone is also devoid of footage. There are photos of the hole-in-one celebrations. Nothing remotely related to the 1st tee or the Tik Tok performance.

Well, that makes the next destination easy. He looks at his list of rooms and roommates. Next stop Room 13. Unlucky for some. Perhaps not. Maybe one of these idiots could simply play ball. With two clowns to deal with rather than just one this might be more difficult. But there is no turning back now. Outside he turns off TKs phone and launches it into the bushes watching the light fade away as it dunked into the undergrowth. He thinks he can see a faint light on the bridge so holds his ground before appearing fully from the fire exit. Yes, someone is there on the bridge, smoking. It seems to take an age, but the light starts to move away back towards the bar.

He approaches the ground floor balcony with some trepidation. Has he counted right. As hoped, the balcony doors are open and curtain slightly ajar. The two of them are in there giggling away. Like two schoolboys caught raiding the spirit cupboard. They start talking about money. More giggling. "Let's have a night cap". He can't tell who is who, which is which. He can't tell Tom from Tom. Flannery has given them a bottle of whiskey. His bottle for closest to the pin.

"Right go and grab a couple of glasses and some ice."

That's it ice. It might be time to put both of these idiots on ice permanently. Just get the footage. Well one gone, one on their own. No time like the present. He walks in brazenly setting the curtain aside still carrying the golf club and towel. He is met by a dazed Tom O' Shea. He has been drinking all day. A little startled. He laughs angrily at the interruption. And No! He doesn't want to hand his phone over. He heads for the door about to open it to show his visitor the exit.

This time with more space to work with. More space to swing, he swings hard. Really puts his hips into it. He felt something brush his face. Blood perhaps. He heard a distinct crunching sound like the sound of timber splitting. He managed to drag the body away from the door. And picks up the phone from Tom O' Sheas hand and luckily it too is open. He is in the middle of a text. He reads it aloud. It was a draft to Tom. Which Tom. So many Toms. His head is a little fuzzy. He checks the contacts and recipient is Tom Noonan. Blah blah blah great times, appreciative, blah blah blah time to move on, hope to remain ... blah blah blah Tom S and Tom T. Instinctively he wants to press send. But he refrains from doing so. No photo. No video. Nothing from the 1st tee. No footage of Triple G. Hang on what's this. A video of Flannery playing out of a bunker. He leaves the ball in there. Sends sand flying. Lots of laughter. "Get that man a bucket and spade." Nothing else from the day.

Well 3 down one to go. He washes the blood splatter from his face. The last of the fourball. Just one left. He didn't have long to wait. Tom O' Toole stumbled into the room wondering why the room was so dark. He had a glass full of ice and two whiskey glasses with him. He is struggling to make sense of his surroundings, so he puts the glasses down on the side table. He takes a step into the room and makes out a Tom O' Shea shaped bundle on the floor. The silly eejit has fallen asleep on the floor. He wonders over to him and crouches down. Wake up you silly bugger. The curtains open slightly, and a glimmer of light reveals that Tom O' Sheas head is split open.

This time, he didn't even bother to ask for the phone. Instead appearing from the darkness, he simply struck Tom T as hard as he could. The man was already leaning over his friend searching for a pulse. O' Toole keeled over but tried to stop himself from pancaking over the body in front of him. He struggled to get up and half turning he looked up behind him just in time to see his attacker bringing another blow down striking him on the head again, and again and again.

Damn, he hadn't expected O' Toole to turn around and stare him full in the eyes. The surprise had meant he added in a couple more blows than he was intending to. He certainly hadn't meant to be so brutal. For reasons of symmetry, he turned Tom O' Toole's body around to match that of Tom O' Shea. Both men looked like they were peacefully sleeping.

Tom T's phone was lit up in his pocket. He wriggled his phone out and there at last there it was, the footage. Several videos. Footage of Triple G doing his thing but with not very complimentary commentary. Delete. Unwanted commentary. Delete. He had worked damn hard to build up a following, strived to work on a persona and to perfect content. Triple G wasn't going to be ridiculed by these jokers. He put the phone in his pocket and removed the sleeves of golf balls. Even though he was wearing gloves he was careful not to touch anything else. He removed the last remaining ball from the open sleeve and one from the, as yet, unopened sleeve, leaving two in that pack.

Time to give them the same treatment as TK.

He left by the same balcony. Golf club, towel and sleeve of balls in hand, packaging in pocket alongside Tom O' Toole's Phone. If he could slip back to his room which was also accessed by ground floor balcony level without waking his roommate this might just work out. He had one final drop off to make. He returned passing by the bunker on the 18th. Even in the pitch back He could make out the shape in the sand. It would stay there until the morning. Flannery's arse on display. Serves you right.

How is that flag up your hole working out for you now.

He walked over the bridge and smashed Tom O' Toole's phone under his foot, before consigning it to its last resting place in the moat. Before venturing back around the perimeter of the complex to his own room he made his way to the holding bay for the locker room and clubs waiting to be cleaned in the locker room.

Searching the various labels, he found what he was looking for, Tom Noonan's name, and he left the club, Michael Flannery's hole-in-one 8-iron club in the bag. He slid the sleeve with two golf balls remaining into the side pocket. An idea suddenly came to him. It might delay things but could be worth it. He opened the shoe bag strung over the clubs. He removed one of the shoes resting inside and returned to the 18th green, shoe on his hand. Reaching over he pressed down in the sand to make a clear imprint in the sand alongside the body as though someone was leaving the sand after making their deposit.

Now, did he have time he wondered. He had got this far so why not. As he found himself back at room 13, he ventured carefully across the balcony. He half expected the bodies to have risen from the dead, ready to exact their revenge on him. He was relieved to see them still laying on the floor where he had left them at peace.

Perhaps he didn't need to do this, but he was invested now. It's not every day you kill four people. It was certainly a first for him. He dipped the shoe in the pool of blood and then reversed so he could leave a print heading out via the balcony leaving another couple of faded prints on his escape leading away from the direction of his room. Back to the locker room. Replace the shoe. Yawn. He was so tired but his heart was racing. He tried to slow his breathing down. Relax. Time for bed.

Creeping back into his room via the balcony which was slightly ajar he realised he was still wearing his gloves and had the towel in his pocket. How had he forgotten to get rid of the towel. But he was so tired. He would get rid of them in the morning. He left them by the side of the bed hidden under clothing. He pulled the doors shut as quietly as he could. He could see movement from the bed next to his. He half undressed and fell into his bed, squirming his way under the covers throwing the cushions on the floor.

Chapter 15

The Blame Game

"My favourite shots are the practice swing and the conceded putt. The rest can never be mastered."

Interviewing a suspect was in many ways an art form, perhaps one that could never be mastered because we all respond to different touch points. Some of us don't respond at all. Eagle had to concede that O' Par was without doubt the most accomplished interviewer he had worked with or seen in action. She somehow managed to be no nonsense and non-confrontational at the same time. She made people want to speak to her. Offered them privacy but never asked for a confession, just sought the truth. And all delivered in her own unique cutting way.

Tom Noonan looked like a defeated man. He looked worried. But perked up, just a little, when he saw the two detectives he had spoken to earlier in the day. At least they hadn't made him feel like a criminal. He had been sat nursing a cup of coffee for the last 20 minutes wondering whether he shouldn't have said some of the things he had said over the last 24 hours or so. He couldn't quite believe what had happened.

In a different room adjacent to where Tom Noonan suddenly envisaged the walls closing in around him, and life behind bars, Laura Yerac, one of Greens examiners from the forensic pathologist's office was taking a closer look at the golf club handed in. She had almost escaped for the day and was due to make a quick pit stop back at the office and then she was heading to her local to catch the pub quiz and if she was lucky the remnants of a roast dinner. Her boyfriend who worked at the pub had promised that he would keep a decent roast aside for her. She was starving. They better had left her a Yorkshire pudding otherwise there would be trouble.

Unfortunately for her, PC Irons had chased her down in the car pack as she was packing an array of equipment away in the SUV. Very quickly she was able to confirm thanks to the use of infrared lighting and a mini sample analysis machine that the burgundy gloop substance trapped in the grooves on the front of the club and the cavity groove on the back of Flannery's 8-iron was indeed blood. There was also another substance on the club within the groove on the head of the club which was bone matter and some soft tissue but that would require further analysis. She made a call back to Green and sent him over some initial pictures of the club, specifically the club head and at his request a number of different shots from different angles of the cavity back of the club which had the grooves around the perimeter. She agreed that she would head straight there and give him the club without delay.

Green and Eagle had agreed the scope of searches required earlier in the day and in addition to the crime scenes and surrounding areas, entrances and exits, the team had already searched the golf bags, room and cars of the Society members so Green was a little perplexed and annoyed that they had missed what was seemingly an easy spot. Later he would find out that Tom Noonan's clubs had been waiting to be cleaned so were not included in the clubs given up for inspection. There had been some confusion with so many Toms in attendance and Tom Noonan's clubs had been cleared and signed off when in fact the clubs inspected had belonged to a different Tom. Which one it didn't really matter.

Green asked Laura Yerac to pass on a message to Eagle before she set off. Her tummy was rumbling and doing cartwheels. That roast dinner seemed a long way off. The message was simply to ask the gentleman who handed in the golf club to give up his golf shoes. The distinctive pattern and markings on the print in the bunker and Room 13 suggested golf shoes and Green thought they might get ahead of the curve. Obviously, he would want to do the same for the whole society but let's start with this particular pair. With Tom Noonan's consent they sent his golf shoes back with Laura Yerac despite the distraction of hunger she still made sure to take photos of the shoes including the sole and imprint for Green and messaged them through ahead of her arrival. Eagle thanked her and asked her to let Green know he would join him later. She couldn't leave soon enough. With each passing moment the chances of a full plate of roast potatoes diminished and as for the Yorkshire pudding, she felt that was already a lost cause. Still, she couldn't help but feel a little sorry for the forlorn figure of Tom Noonan who had gone very pale and sat with his head in his hands, almost as if he was holding it in place.

Eagle had intended to make the Pathologist office his final stop of the day but that depended on how things went here with Tom Noonan. Eagle was fully aware that Fin, his Labrador, was sat at home. He would be hungry and would probably leave a protest poo on the floor if he wasn't let out soon and fed.

"Am I under arrest"? Tom Noonan asked meekly.

"Why would you think that Mr Noonan. We just need to ask you some questions" Eagle answered in his most friendly tone.

O' Par stepped in "Tom, can we get you anything. I for one am gonna grab a cup of tea while I have the chance."

"Oh right yeah some tea." The coffee he had nursed was giving him heartburn but that could have been stress induced.

DI Flog was in attendance and a couple of officers were also milling around and one of the young PCs was sent to get some more tea.

"Any biscuits going" Eagle's request sounded more like a demand.

"Look Mr Noonan. It's been a difficult time, but we need to ask you some questions. Not just because of the club found in your bag".

Noonan sat upright not prepared to throw in the towel just yet. "That bloody club has nothing to do with me. The first I knew of it in my bag was out on the course today".

"Woah, hold up Mr Noonan.". Eagle remained calm. "At the moment you are not under caution or arrest.. at the moment all we want to do is have a chat with you."

O' Par offered an olive branch, "Look Tom we know you didn't have your clubs overnight. You left them in the locker room ready to be cleaned ahead of today's round". Noonan nodded but before he could add anything O' Par continued "and we know that Michael Flannery spent most of the evening with his golf club toasting it because of the Hole-in-one." She let that linger.

“He did that alright” Tom Noonan was growing in confidence.

“What we really need to know from you Tom is what you knew about Michael Flannery’s job offers to Tom O’ Shea and Tom O’ Toole, they both worked for you didn’t they?” And I guess we also want to know why you said the things you did about wrapping your club round Tom O Keefe’s head.”

Tom Noonan was about to defend himself. He was about to speak up. Instead, he ended up shrugging and offering his hands out as if he was about to beg for his life. The last thing he needed at that precise moment in time was Eagle chipping in.

“While we are at it, we should probably find out what you thought of your former business partner, Michael Flannery buying Tom S and Tom T’s support for his campaign for Captaincy.”

Tom squirmed in his seat. O’ Par was considering letting him speak.

Instead, she offered “God Tom it doesn’t look good. The four guys you seem to have had more than one altercation with or reason to be angry with, well they are dead.”

“I didn’t do it” was all Tom offered. “It’s ridiculous. I am not a killer. I couldn’t. I was angry. I am a good boss. Treated them really well. They would be making the worst mistake of their lives joining that eejit Flannery but, if that’s their choice. Sure I felt betrayed but come on … murder.”

Awkward pause. Eagle and O' Par glance up at each other. Noonan looks as though he might cry.

"I didn't do it".

"We know" Jenny O' Par puts a hand on his shoulder. Tea has arrived. "Ah you know my mam always says life is like a cup of tea, it's all in how you make it." She smiled at Tom Noonan and he tried to smile back.

"Tell us what happened last night Tom. What you can remember."

Tom spills all. Finding out about the captaincy. Overhearing the job offers. He knew something was up. Flannery's Hole-in-one. He is a wind up. The man is insufferable but for all that we were mates. A lot of history. I would always have a drink with him. He would forever make me mad. But for all that I loved the guy and wouldn't even do him harm. He tells them about the conciliatory cigar and how the two of them were going to have a smoke on the bridge. He tells them that TK had let slip to Seamus who let slip to Tom Noonan that Flannery was offering his Toms (O' Shea and O' Toole) incentives to support his bid for captaincy. That upset him. The captaincy had meant a lot to him. Not. Not enough to kill he added.

He went to find TK. Flannery had gone AWOL. He caught TK going to his room. The two had words. Yes he did threaten to shove a club up his hole and that he would do something or rather to his bollox. But TK was too drunk to give a shit. Noonan gave up on him and decided to go find Flannery, have a smoke and tell him he could have the damn captaincy if it meant that much to him. Except Flannery was nowhere to be found. Some of the guys were talking to a group of women at the bar. Some were running around playing silly buggers with cardboard cutouts from the wedding fayre. Some had already gone to bed. The card game had finished. Pat was saying his goodnights. JC too. Gabe was going strong but had gone out for some fresh air. Noonan went out and had a smoke. On the bridge by himself. He could already smell the scent of cigar in the air and he saw the remains of a cigar on the ground, embers burning out. Maybe Flannery had already been out. Maybe he was too pissed to hold on to his cigar. Dropped it. Yes it would be unlike him. Tom Noonan enjoyed his cigar. He went to bed. JC was still awake when Noonan turned up ready for bed.

"I didn't do it. I didn't hurt anyone. I didn't kill anyone."

"We know you didn't do it." O' Par reassured him.

"But did you see anything else while you were outside on the bridge." Eagle asked.

"No not really it was so quiet. Ok, I thought I saw a brief flash of light in the bushes and a noise. Just before I left. Something flashed up and then it was gone. I waited to see what it was. Nothing. So I left."

"Is that everything" Eagle asked.

"Well one more thing, not only am I not a killer. I am also not an idiot. If I did murder someone, or indeed 4 people, I certainly wouldn't be foolish enough to leave the damn murder weapon in my own golf bag."

O' Par looked up at Eagle. "You owe me dinner." Eagle shook his head. Noonan was lost.

"So am I under arrest? Am I a suspect."

Eagle looked at his phone and the message that had flashed through from Green. 'Match on the shoe prints. Those golf shoes match the print in Room 13 but smells iffy'.

"No you are not under arrest Mr Noonan. Go and join the others but be careful. Someone has gone to great lengths in between killing 4 people to pin the blame firmly on you."

Chapter 16

Joyride into the Past

"The only thing a golfer needs is more daylight".

Sometimes there simply weren't enough hours in the day as far as Green was concerned to get through all he needed to. Death didn't respect boundaries or acknowledge time. Death was relentless. Perhaps it was simply the line of business he was in or more that he had an insatiable desire for answers. The certainty of death in contrast to the uncertainty of the hour of death is a source of grief throughout life and a source of irritation to Green. But then again uncertainty can be fascinating.

"Do you know Fuzzy Zoeller, won at his first attempt at playing the Masters. His first time playing the Masters at Augusta. He claimed he barely had a thought in his head over any shot throughout the tournament. He figured that his local caddy knew the course a lot better than him. He put his faith in the caddy. Put his hand out and played whatever the caddy gave him. He would ask how hard to hit it. The caddy would tell him and Fuzzy would swing."

“That’s great." Golf, my favourite subject Eagle thought to himself. "Thanks for the info.” Eagle was dressed in his forensic tuxedo as he liked to call it. All dressed up with nowhere to go. He stood a little away from the table where the body of Michael Flannery lay. Over the years he had become more comfortable with attending postmortems. Perhaps comfortable was the wrong word. He was less freaked out than he once would have been.

“Right so in that case can I suggest that you stop trying to tell me how to do my job and interrupting at everything I say. I am the expert. I am the caddy. And you well …your Fuzzy Zoeller about to take all the credits for my hard work.”

“Ok I got you Doc.” Eagle knew that Green hated being addressed as Doc.

"The wounds on all four bodies are from the same weapon. The groove imprint even where only partial contact was made, match the same weapon." The same golf club. Flannery’s 8-iron as brought in last night. "There are multiple traces of blood on the club but you will have to wait for the lab to confirm."

"There was also some brain matter caught up in the hosel of the club". Eagle looked lost. So, Green explained it was the neck of the club. Eagle found that the secret to surviving the postmortem, sitting in on one as opposed to standing outside looking in was small shallow breaths. He would always do his best to pay attention and follow Green enthusiastically pointing out points of interest even if that meant he occasionally got acquainted with internal organs or worse ended up close and personal with wounds he would otherwise do his best to avoid. It was easier to look at a photo afterwards in the debrief than see flesh, well in the flesh.

He could sense they were coming to the end of proceedings. Not a moment too soon. The most exciting development for him other than confirmation of the murder weapon was the golf balls. On the other side of the autopsy room four golf balls, all Titleist Pro V1s sat in individual containers. Each retrieved from the dead bodies of the four men who arrived yesterday from Chorus Hills. Eagle was excited to hear that Green had discovered wool-blend fabrics on each of the balls and in the mouths of the three Toms. The same fabrics were found in Flannery too after the ball was removed from his anus. Eagle shuddered. Green explained. These fabrics, this blend is commonly found on gloves. Not just any gloves. Touch screen gloves. They have a special PVC coating. Touchscreen compatible. Basically, they allow you to wear gloves and still use your phone or tablet. Eagle felt a twinge of hope. We need to find those gloves.

"Now what else do you need to know" Green muttered almost to himself. He looked like he was finishing up. Michael Flannery was being dismissed. "We found traces of blood on the bridge on the 18th…That's where Flannery was struck it would seem……" Green let that linger. “We are dealing with a strong individual. The brut force of the strikes is utter pandemonium. Three of them have been effectively downed by one blow. Tom O’Keefe has been hit several times not always cleanly and judging by the bruising attempted to block the attack. He is the only one who has been attacked with both sides of the club. The other three have been struck with the back of the club so impact has been from the back cavity and the heavier motif resting within the back cavity."

“Any significance in that” Eagle enquired.

Green considered this question and then looked momentarily like he was thinking whether to hold back or not. “Well, it could be because it’s the heavier side of the club …. Or …”

“Go on” Eagle nudged him.

“Or it could suggest a lefty.”

“A left hander.”

“Yeah Phil Mickelson. Old lefty. The angle of attack leans towards that explanation too.”

“Phil Mickelwho?” Eagle scrunched up his face.

“Christ, Eagle you really are a hopeless case.”

“Hey no fair. I have been reading up. I know all about Ian Woosnam.”

“Well then you are bang up to date. Look let’s get cleaned up and I will go through the photos and pictures with you on the prints and blood splatter. I will show you the club and what I mean by the angle of attack and how you might hold the club and swing it."

Stripped out of his forensic Tux, Eagle put in place his usual post postmortem protocol and opened up a little bag of sweets breathing in the smell of gummies and sugar. He grabbed a handful and shoved them in his mouth. That felt better. Then he sprayed a dash of cologne on his wrist and dabbed a little under his nose and enjoyed briefly inhaling the scent to remove the smell of death, the smell of not existing from his nostrils. He checked his phone. The Commissioner had already left a message for an update. Ignore that one. Another answerphone message. Julian from Chorus Hills. Pro shop reported a late-night theft, well joyride, on the night of the murders. They have CCTV footage. Eagle thought for a moment. The murders all took place on site. At the complex or right under their noses the 18th Green and Bunker being just yards away from the bar and Dining room. So, a buggy wouldn't have been needed unless someone had something to hide, something to dump out on the course. He listened to the message again. The buggy was returned minutes later. Not the work of kids out for a joyride.

He checked his text messages. One from O' Par. 'Wake up you lazy gobshite. We have work to do. Am at the course'. Good morning to you too he thought.

Green offered him a coffee and some biscuits. Eagle gave him the thumbs up as he called O' Par. She answered straight away.

"Commissioner Jenny O 'Par speaking how may I help you".

Eagle ignored her. Don't give her the satisfaction "O' Par, good morning my little ray of sunshine."

"Ok" she interrupted … "who are you and where have you dumped the body of my boss."

"Jenny"… slight pause, for once no interruption, "do you think you could head over to the pro shop and pick up some footage. One of the buggies went missing Saturday night briefly, quite late … it was taken. Seems they have their own cameras, separate to the complex. And there is something caught on film."

"Sure… but like what are we expecting here."

"Well they got someone caught on film and a picture… maybe something, you can go smooth over so that Julian knows how seriously we investigate crime and then send it to that geeky guy from the tech department that is in love with you."

"You mean Geek… agh sure you can't blame him. Doesn't have eyes in his head."

"Yeah him… he may well have eyes somewhere behind those milk bottles."

"Don't be mean you shitehawk. I will have you know that Graeme Pratt is the best there is. When it comes to corrupt files, mobile phones, fuzzy pictures…"

“Fuzzy … don’t talk to me about fuzzy I am stood watching your bestie Green juggle internal organs and giving me a lecture about some golfer called Fuzzy”.

“There’s a golfer called Fuzzy … she asked in disbelief”.

“Really, that’s what is weird about my statement … not the juggling organs.”

“Sure I rarely see him without someone’s insides in his hands.”

“Whatever floats your boat Jenny”…

“What are you doing” Eagle asked.

“Well right now I am in the trophy room… grabbing a coffee and a bacon sarnie. Yer man Julian was delighted to see us again…and offered me breakfast to get me out of the way. Other than that waiting for our guys to all gather together for brunch before they head off…oh I spoke to Gabe, low key, he hasn’t seen any footage other than the final edits. Said he doesn’t get involved in that side of things. Leaves it to Daniel James.”

“Interesting. I bet Julian was delighted, all you need now is Captain Bogey to turn up and offer to crack the case open.”

“Agh sure he can’t do any worse than you can he.”

“How do you fancy traffic detail … O’ Par” Eagle laughed.

“Sure, if it means some time away from you then sign me up ….” She raised her eyes up to heaven and her eyes focused on the Trophy commemorative boards. She was stood in front of the junior boards and there it was jumping out at her "junior club championship - The Manning Trophy 2014 and 2015 Daniel James. That name. Seeing it up in lights. It can't be. Daniel James. He had said he was a golfer. But not anymore. And he lives in London so was not exactly a local boy.

"Jen … Jen are you there"?

"Oh yeah sure thing boss … will head over there now."

"It's probably nothing. Last thing we need checking out some dickheads out joyriding… but so help me God if I have one more call from Commissioner letting me know what Rupert Fucking Bogey thinks well then, we might have another body left out on the course and I won't leave any organs for Green to play with."

"Aha" O' Par instinctively replied though she was distracted.

"But equally odd that on the night of the murders someone takes a late-night drive and comes back moments later."

"Could have got rid of something."

"Exactly, Right catch you later…"

The junior Championship 8 years ago 2015 Daniel James … It couldn't be. Slight coincidence. She wasn't one for believing in coincidences. Well perhaps the pro would know. That was her next stop anyway. The pro shop was quiet. There was a TV on in the corner and a young man, assistant pro badge adorning his polo, stood behind the desk typing away on the computer. O' Par introduced herself and explained why she was there. “Oh, right sure let me get Clive. Releasing footage. Above my pay grade I am afraid.” He contacts Clive. Looks around the room searching for a job to do “He is on his way. Won’t be long.”

“Thanks a million.”

O’ Par studied the assistant pro dressed in blue trousers and a pink under armour polo trying to age him. He might be the same age or perhaps a little younger than Daniel James. So, she asks the question. “Yep, everyone knew Daniel. He played for the England Junior team. Equalled the course record here at just 15.”

“Is he still around now? Does he play?” she asked innocently.

“Err” the young man became a little flustered picking up a pack of golf balls so he had something to do with his hands. “You will need to speak to Clive. He has been here forever”. Clive, it seemed a strong name for an old club pro. Clive the old pro who knew everyone and everything. And then he appeared Clive. Just as she imagined he would look. Well turned out. Coiffed salt and pepper hair with a deep tan.

“Daniel, yeah everyone knew Daniel. what do you want to know. He was a good kid. Super talented golfer. Destined for big things. A little intense.” O’ Par didn’t offer to interrupt and flashed a smile so he continued.

“He could spend hours repeating the same shot. Over and over. Perfecting it. He could just block out all the noise and focus on the task in hand when it came to practice. He was all about the preparation. A perfectionist.” O’ Par nodded to show she was following and allowed Clive to carry on.

“Well, his problem was that he could lose his cool and it was game over. A volcanic eruption. Troubled upbringing. Always fighting at home. In and out of Foster homes. He knew how to handle himself. Such a shame.” Clive Hillmax shook his head. “He loved this place. You know Tiger Woods got his first hole in one when he was 8. Daniel scored one here when he was 7.”

O’ Par was ready to burst. “Ok, you got me. What was such a shame”?

“Well we were playing a county match against another club and he lost his shit. He was 15. It was just a few weeks after he equalled the course record here. He is playing against this kid two years older. It kicks off. They have a dispute about a putt. The other guy is tending the flag for Daniel and doesn’t remove it in time … Daniel’s ball ends up hitting the pin. Two shot penalty. Back in the day. Not anymore of course.” Clive shakes his head again. “The kid says it was a mistake and the flag got stuck but the rules are the rules and so he takes a one-shot lead.”

“They are playing match play” O’ Par asks. Clive nods and continues with his story.

“As they walk to the next tee Daniel catches the kid and his dad who had been caddying for him laughing and fist bumping so he breaks the kid’s jaw.”

“Nooo. Stop. At 15?” O’ Par is shocked.

“Yep. The dad starts to kick off so Daniel attacks him too. Breaks his nose with the flagpole. He has marched back to the green and brought the flagpole with him to use as a weapon. He is caught beating them both with a flag… and has to be dragged away. And that is that. He is Dragged away. Juvenile courts … thrown off the England team. No more golf.”

“Christ!”

“He ended up in juvenile detention. It was a real shame. This place was his home. He lived here. Knew every corridor, pathway, blade of grass.”

“Would you have a photo of Daniel.”

“There will be plenty around the clubhouse. Look in the member’s bar. There will be one above the coffee station. He is holding the junior county trophy up. You can’t miss him. We had to take the individual ones down.”

O’ Par can barely concentrate. It can’t be the same Daniel James. Can it? First things first. Let’s see the camera footage.

It's 3 am. Who the feck is going for a little joyride. The image is grainy. The joyrider is dressed in black. Hood up. Unaware of the camera but still wary to keep his hood up. She had the digital files sent to the tech team and sent the Geek a personalised message to do his thing. She types 'Hey G! Will buy you a drink if you can get me a pic of his face. Or a distinctive Tattoo'...

She takes a picture on her phone and tried to zoom in. The joyrider is carrying something. Holding something like he is smuggling something under his top or maybe something is wrapped up in his top.

Well, it's in the hands of the Geek now. Let him work his magic. With that little diversion done O' Par thanks Clive and the nameless assistant pro and heads over to the members bar to check out some old photos. She heads straight for the coffee station. And sure enough there it is a giant photo of the boys' junior team 2014 county champions. She pours herself a coffee while she is here. The boy with the biggest smile taking centre stage is being held aloft while holding onto a giant trophy. He had a mop of unmistakable blonde hair partly covered by the lid of the trophy that he is holding in his other hand. It's Daniel James. The Daniel James. Tik Tok content editor. Triple G Daniel James. Cute Daniel James. Too young for her Daniel James.

Feck. Did that change anything? So, he used to play here and knew the venue. So he might have been a bit violent in his past and got in a little bit of trouble, did that change anything. Gabe still confirmed that Daniel was tucked up in bed fast asleep when he came up. Attacking someone with a flagpole was very different to shoving it up someone's hole. Wasn't it?

"Oh, Hi Jenny isn't it. Sorry I mean DCI O' Par" He was the last person she expected to see. She was startled.

"You haven't got my work phone and laptop have you".

"Oh err I am afraid I haven't… we can get them back to you later today Mr James."

"Daniel is fine" …

"Oh, right sure Daniel."

"It's me … a younger version of me. I saw you looking."

"I can see that."

"You never said you played here… or knew the place …"

"Well you never asked … I told you I used to play .. that was a long time ago. Another world. Another lifetime."

"But you could have told us" O' Par urged.

"I could … I don't think it was relevant … part of my life I have put behind me" Daniel James shrugged nonchalantly.

"Right so what are you doing in in here? Reminiscing about old times."

"Well to be honest I am a bit worried about Gabe.... I think he may have seen and heard some footage which might have upset him."

"Gabe is missing?" Interesting she thought to herself as she spoke to him earlier and he insisted he hadn't seen any footage.

"And I haven't seen him since this morning when he was speaking to Tom. The one that is always angry. So I thought I would see if I could find him".

"Agh I am sure he will turn up."

"I hope so he seemed pretty restless in the night."

"Fame"...

"I know sometimes if helps to be a nobody. Slip into the shadows."

"Is that one you too?" O' Par points to a photo of crowd stood around a tee box and a solitary blonde boy in the middle holding his pose at the top of his swing.

"Yep that's me."

"A cack hander."

"Exactly a lefty. Prob why me and Gabe get on so well."

Chapter 17

Being No.1

"Golf, like measles, should be caught young."

Daniel James had been playing golf since he was 5 years old. He caught the bug when a neighbour saw fit to offer him some respite and take him down the range to accompany him on his practice days. The range became the course. His mum was only too pleased to have the boy out from under her feet and it also meant he had time away from the violence and anger that permeated their family life. His behaviour improved. He was less explosive or reactive the arguments that surrounded him at home. He had fallen in love with the sport and dedicated every spare second to it. When most boys his age would be dreaming of superheroes or of scoring the winning goal in a cup final. Daniel James was firming up swing thoughts or working out his schedule of events to capture all the main US events. Most of all he imagined wining the Open Championship and who he would thank in his speech. It was a short speech. By the time he was ten he even included a line in there to thank his middle finger for sticking up for him when he needed it most. It wasn't that he was ill tempered he just had a low threshold for people pissing him off.

Tiger Woods spent 683 weeks at world No.1. 281 weeks of that total was spent as consecutive world No.1. Top of the tree. Golf is an easy game, but it really is quite hard to play. It takes practice. Playing golf at the top level takes more than just practice, it needs dedication, commitment. Daniel James had that dedication. At least at one point, when everything was going well. Before his world crashed around him, golf was going to be his way out, his career, his everything. He had a new family at Chorus Hills. One that wouldn't let him down. And one day he would tee it up alongside Tiger Woods probably at the Open Championship. Finally, Daniel James would be content.

That didn't quite happen. Life has a way of biting you in the backside and interrupting even the best laid plans. Dedication only takes you so far especially when you have your own internal demons to master. He had been told by his neighbour, a kind natured Norwegian gentleman with a love of golf that the best remedy for a bad temper was a long walk. And golf helped him achieve this. He unleashed the anger he felt inside on ball striking and the walk did the rest. He would finish each round with a new-found sense of peace. Ready to do it all again. Ready to handle whatever lay in wait at home. He would be back at the course at the next opportunity.

When golf gave up on Daniel James, he lost his love for the game. However, the urge to pick up a club again was slowly returning. He might not be in the running for qualifying for the Open Championship any time soon but Triple G had restored his faith in the game and in humankind. Daniel James was worried. Genuinely worried. Gabe had not been himself. And now he had disappeared.

....

Eagle had a missed call from O' Par. He tried calling back but no answer. He typed out a message as quickly as his fingers allowed "Am heading to the course. Our killer is a left hander who wears touchscreen gloves. Prob. Can you find out who amongst our group is a lefty". That was one of the longest messages he had ever written on his phone. He was proud of himself. It had taken less than 5 minutes to type too. He set off for the course wondering if he passed a coffee shop on the way. He was peckish and by now a safe distance away from the Mortuary his appetite had returned for breakfast. Sweets and biscuits even for him were not a hearty breakfast.

O' Par had already asked Floggy to get together a search team after reviewing the footage. She could tell that, thanks to some logistical advice from good old dependable Clive, the joyrider on the buggy left in the direction leading away from the clubhouse down the 10th hole. He or she had returned lighter than when they left and that wasn't because they had stopped to have a shit in the woods. Whatever bundle of contraband was being cuddled around their midriff had been left out there on the course.

The Commissioner had not been best pleased to find out that Tom Noonan hadn't been arrested and that the case was still ongoing. He was probably going to be even less pleased about the idea of sending more officers to the course on mass. Which is probably why Eagle agreed it was a good idea and authorised Floggy to carry on, still unable to get hold of O' Par.

It was certainly possible that someone with something that they didn't want to be seen with had taken a trip out to the course and dumped the offending articles in the unknown. On top of that following Tom Noonan's revelation that he saw something light up in and then disappear in the woodland to the edge of the 18th Green neighbouring the clubhouse and car park it seemed sensible to search there too. He tried O' Par again, but number was temporarily unavailable. He resisted the temptation to tell the lady apologising in the message to fuck off. Instead, he rang DI Flog and confirmed that while he hadn't spoken to Jenny O' Par yet they should initiate two searches. O' Par would fill him in upon arrival, but the second search was to look for a mobile phone in the immediate woodland to the right of the 18th Green as you approach the clubhouse.

He drove deep in thought, half looking out for a cafe to make a quick pit stop, trying to put the pieces together. Yesterday the frogmen had found Michael Flannery's phone in the pond on the 19th. They had also found the remains of Tom T's phone too. It had taken a bit of a beating. The glorified moat didn't give up much else, some solar panel lights and of all things a putter. Green was delighted at this little bit of news and had insisted on telling a story about a well-known character, a golfer known as the Walrus, Craig Stadler, back in the days before any golfer had seen the inside of a gym, who when asked why he was using a new putter replied that it was because the old one didn't float too well. The putter had been quickly dismissed as a possible weapon.

Tom O Keefe's phone was missing. Tom O' Sheas phone had been left on him. He had been in the middle of a text, as it was, a draft, an unsent text intended for none other than Tom Noonan about to give him the bad news. Convenient. Three missing phones, two of which had now been found badly damaged. Time would tell what the tech guys could do with the damaged phones. O' Par swore the Geek, and his team could make anything work. Eagle didn't hold out much hope. One device still missing. It certainly made sense to assume that whatever else was going on the Killer had been looking for something on the victims phones. Small wool-blend fibres coated with PVC found on the phone belonging to Tom O' Shea, matched the fibres found on the golf balls and victims. The person responsible for the murders had interfered with the phone that was left behind. Perhaps they had been satisfied that there was nothing worth destroying on Tom O' Sheas phone. But the phones were crucial.

Phones, Lefties and touchscreen gloves Eagle thought to himself. Slim pickings. They would need more. The Society were due to meet for a late breakfast or was it an early lunch. Eagle wasn't a fan of the term brunch. He hadn't had any abuse from O' Par for at least 12 hours and though he wouldn't admit it he was missing her.

....

Back at the Course, there was a flurry of activity. Set up for a wedding reception was in full flow. Not only were the reception rooms being used but a large marquee was being set up in the lawns to the side of the Spa where usually lunch would be served to those in their robes.

People. The last thing he needed. He didn't feel like speaking. He had contemplated going for a little walk along the course. Yesterday's golf was subdued. Dinner was pleasant. There had been some stories shared and golfing mishaps involving the four fallen members. Plenty of drink consumed. After all it was a send-off, well of sorts. It could have been a sombre affair. Jed was delighted not just with his hole-in-one but with his overall performance which surely had meant he had won the weekend competition over course of the two days. A village somewhere was definitely missing an idiot.

The morning had come, and Jonny Rosewait and Joseph Mcilroy had already spoken with Captain Keith to agree to cancel any formal prizegiving. Instead, when this terrible ordeal was over and someone had been brought to Justice they would put up a memorial cup in honour of the four men. It didn't bear thinking about. Mcilroy, in particular, tried to put it in context. How did a simple gathering of friends assembled to go play some golf turn into this. Bad timing, he surmised. No accounting for bumping into some homicidal maniac.

He had overheard Keith asking whether they thought it could be one of us… Jonny had tried to relax him. "Don't be silly and you were too busy with your cardboard cut-out girlfriend."

Joseph had chipped in "mind you … I would watch your back if you come across that lady from the Wedding Conference. "She definitely was not a fan of yours" Rosewait followed up.

Then he saw saw DCI O' Par join them. He heard her ask them who in the Society played left-handed.

"That depends" Mcilroy offered intrigued.

"We only have one lefty this weekend" Rosewait added.

"And he is right-handed. Like Lefty. Big Phil. A right hander that learned to play left-handed."

"Agh guys sometime today" O' Par pleaded.

"Gabe"… the gents replied in unison.

Keith joined the party. He looked a little more refreshed than the previous morning. "I didn't know Gabe was right-handed" Captain Keith declared.

"Yeah, plays left-handed something to do with his hurling days back in Ireland." O' Par could certainly envisage that scenario. Hurling was a big thing where she came from. It was her turn to go all Columbo.

"Just one more thing Gents" she asked.

"Does Gabe wear gloves?"

"Not in this weather" Keith was quick to respond.

“Or ever” Mcilroy added.

“Eczema” Rosewait interrupted. “Doesn’t even wear a glove on the course…which is rare.”

She excused herself not seeing him in the background. Damn it he thought. Was he going to be found out. She was very interested in him all of a sudden. Anyone could have seen from Triple G’s profile and videos that he was a lefty. He wasn’t just a lefty. He was a right-handed lefty who generated a phenomenal club head speed for a man of his age. He was strong. He was fit. He was at the height of his fame and he couldn’t afford any mishaps or jumps to derail the commercial juggernaut, the cash cow. Any threat to Gabe was a threat to Triple G.

He listened as she spoke with another officer on the phone. Stuey. Well Stuey and her were going to do a sweep of the woods down the tenth and the woodland rough adjacent to the 18th Green. Fuck he thought.

He had nearly messed up. Thankfully he woke a little before 3 am. He had been restless. Well, you would be after doing what he had just done. He jumped out of bed. Composed himself. His roommate was dead to the world. Asleep. Breathing. That was a relief. He slipped on some clothes. Carefully selected his hoody. Best not to be seen. Picked up the bundle he left by his bed. Bloody Towel. Flattened packaging from a pack of Titleist Pro V1s and gloves. He put the gloves on. Don't leave any prints.

Making his way down to the buggy shed to the side of the pro shop he knew exactly which buggy still had keys in. The pro shop had been closed when they tried to return it. He slid into the front seat. Hood up. He held the towel and packaging wrapped up on the middle of the towel close to him. He didn't want to lose them in the dark. He looked around. Scratched his head. He was hot in the hoody. No sign of cameras just as he thought. He sped off down the tenth. To think he nearly neglected to tidy up after himself. Drive. Drive. Stop. This will do. He jumps out of the cart. It's dark. The woodland is thick. Brambles reaching out. He lights the way with his phone. The gloves work perfectly. His phone responds and he finds a route into the woods. No not deep enough. He ventures in further. He finds a felled tree. The inside of the remaining stump is hollow. He puts the towel and the packaging within in the hollow. There. That's the end of that for a while. He quickens his pace. Back to the buggy. Spin it round and floors it back to the buggy shed. Even reverses it in risking the few seconds of noise that reverse gear introduces. Done. Shit. Shit he thinks the gloves. He opens the little glove box. Why not he thinks. Leave them in there. Who knows when they might surface. He shuts the glove box with his knees. Careful not to touch it with his exposed hands.

And back to bed.

……………………..

Eagle had already passed by the entrance to the McDonalds drive thru at the roundabout. He had just passed through Uckfield when he felt an intense hunger. He contemplated turning round. Too late. He soldiered on to the golf course. There was a flurry of activity upon his arrival. It looked like a group of golfers, wedding party and police officers had all gathered to do battle at reception. Eagle spotted Julian running around like he might have lost his mind. O' Par was there and together with Floggy they guided the officers away from the mass gathering. He made his way over to them watching as the colour slowly returned to Julian's cheeks.

"Jaysus, the dead arose and appeared to man" O' Par greeted her boss.

"Jenny" he nodded.

“I need to talk to you about Daniel James” she spoke guiding him away from the officers assembled around DI Floggy awaiting further instructions.

“Ok Ok I give you my blessing …Eagle replied suppressing a little chortle, “as long as his mum and dad give permission and you have him back by 10.30.”

“Agh you Amadan.”

Eagle apologised and filled her in on the postmortems and Green’s findings. In turn she let him know what she knew about Daniel James.

“I don’t like it Jenny. I don’t like that he held that back from us.”

O’ Par Shrugged. She tended to agree.

“I also don’t like it that a golf club used to kill 4 people helpfully appeared in the bag of the one guy everyone thinks might just be angry enough to go around killing people. I don’t like it that the same guy’s golf shoes which he was most certainly not wearing in the evening match the prints in the sandpit…

“Bunker”…

“And in room 13. Green is convinced that the pressure on the shoes wasn’t right. They didn’t give us the print you would expect.”

“I don’t follow.”

“His explanation is that that they were used like a paint brush to create a picture. Dipped in the blood and used”.

O’ Par looked deep in thought. Something was distracting her. Eagle continued.

“I also don’t like it that the Pro V1s balls won by Flannery also turned up in Noonan bag. He is no fool. And he is no killer.”

Jenny O’ Par takes a deep intake of breath. “We only have one lefty. And Daniel James seems to think that Gabe has seen some footage which has upset him. He has gone AWOL.”

“Remember Flannery is key. Don’t juggle too many balls.” Eagle reminds her.

“Gabe is 70 years of age” he adds.

“Agh sure killing is a young man’s game.”

“Well, I am not sure about that…but” he stops himself. Floggy interrupts.

“Sir. We are ready to go. Both teams in place.”

“Right let’s get this ramshackle show of misfits on the road.”

“I think you need to know” Floggy went on “that we, or rather the station has had a distress call. Gabe’s granddaughter has suggested she is worried about him.”

Eagle perked up. “What… what do you mean”.

“Exact words, he messaged her to say he is worried he might get found out. He has something to confess.”

“Fuck a Duck” Eagle announces. “Where is Gabe??”

“I told you Sir” O’ Par replied impatiently. “He has gone out on the course to clear his mind”.

The Geek has come through. Eagle and O’ Par look at each other as their phones ping at the same time. The download takes an age. The photo appears. ‘Not a tattoo I am afraid but a logo’. The closeup of the dark hoody is grainy then the focus zooms in on a logo. The unmistakable insignia of Triple G’s logo reflecting the light.

Chapter 18

Dizzy heights on the Range

"One of the most fascinating things about golf is how it reflects the cycle of life. No matter what you shoot – the next day you have to go back to the first tee and begin all over again and make yourself into something."

Beginning all over again was something Daniel James knew all too well. He had rebuilt a life for himself and was slowly rehabilitating himself back into a world where he felt most comfortable. You get knocked down. You suffer setbacks. You start all over again.

He didn't want to start back at the first tee however. After everything he had done maybe he could just for once get a leg up. Maybe he could start from the tenth. Put the front nine behind him and start afresh on the back nine. The cycle of life had given him a new bike to ride. A big part of his success was Triple G. Gabe. The two got on well. Away from the camera, Gabe genuinely cared for him and told him he was family. Bloody hell family. Something Daniel hadn't had for a long time. He wasn't going to let him do anything silly.

O’ Par caught Daniel James at the pro shop. “Where are you off to?”

“I am gonna find Gabe” he replied defiantly. “His granddaughter Eva has messaged me. She is worried and I think I know where he is.”

“Ok I will come with you.” Elsewhere the grounds were already being searched and Eagle had asked for more support to corner off all exits.

The Geek messaged again. It read ‘Stand by. Two more coming through.’ Interesting. O’ Par jumped in alongside Daniel James. She barely sat her bum on the seat before he floored it.

“Where are we going”. She asked.

“Well Gabe loved the view over the valley. It’s the 4th hole. We both agreed it’s a great place to think. Hopefully that’s where he is.”

Her phoned pinged. It’s another picture message from G. It won’t download. she can’t view it. They are already 500 yards and counting away from the clubhouse. Catch you later G.

Eagle is trying to coordinate the search while also looking to keep officers posted around the complex. His phone pings and he opens the photo sent through from the Geek. Jenny was not wrong. He is a genius. He has isolated the joyrider from the dark and focused on the split second showing the joyrider lifting his hood to scratch his head. The unmistakable mop of blonde, almost white, hair making the most fleeting of appearances and the realisation stabs Eagle in the eye. He has just given O' Par the nod to team up with him to search for Gabe. He has just let her jump in with Daniel James. A fucking homicidal maniac who kills indiscriminately with one blow. He puts out a message for all officers on the scene. "Suspect is a young man, blonde hair, 25 year-old Daniel James". Not a 70-year-old dancing Grandad he thinks to himself.

Ping. Another message from the Geek. A Slow motion video. In the dark the joyrider opens the glove box and removes gloves and uses their elbows to shut them away in the glove box. If he wasn't about to give himself a hernia, he would have given the geek a little round of applause. He would usually want to get hands on the gloves without delay. Instead. They need to find O' Par and Daniel James.

Eagle hollers at Floggy who is approaching him "Get out on the course and find O' Par."

Pulling up behind the green on the 4th hole.... there he was. Gabe. Stood on the 5th tee resting on a handrail looking down into the valley. Jaysus she couldn't quite believe it. How had he done it. 70 years of age. Best get this over and done with. He looked like he might just top himself if she didn't intervene.

Daniel James let her approach Gabe with him keeping his distance. Gabe turned around. "It's ok G!" Daniel James shouts out.

"It's alright, Gabe, it's alright... I am just here to understand" O' Par puts it out there.

"Oh right.... I didn't think the police would get involved." Gabe is perplexed.

"You didn't" O' Par admires his resolve.

"Well, no ... I mean it was an accident."

"Hmmmm" O' Par adds "even so ... 4 accidents"...

"It was a simple mistake."

"Agh now Gabe would you cop on ... you can't go around killing people".

"What" Gabe looks startled ... "Killing!"

"Gabe… why don't you tell me what you are sorry about…." She thinks he is about to run. Can she chase down a 70-year-old man. She is an ultra-marathon runner. She has got this.

"Well, the extra club" Gabe looks like he is going to cry. …. "I had an extra club in my bag, caught on camera… the new driver we were trying out. I put it back in the bag."

"Oh, Jaysus Mary Mother of God…. That's what you are upset about. Are you for real."

She looked at her phone. Zero coverage, no reception. Two messages. Two messages waiting to download from the Geek. She holds her phone up and wriggles it around as if she knows this trick conjures up reception. Another message comes through from Eagle. Maybe it did work. Short and not so sweet. "It's Daniel James. Get away from him. on way". Something in the way she looked up from her phone at him gave the game away. It's ok it was only a matter of time he thought. At least out here for the time being he was free.

"Daniel …we need to head back" she guides Gabe back to the buggy.

"No Jenny I am going to need you to stay here with Gabe" Daniel James has a defiant look upon his face.

“And Jenny I am going to need your phone.” She doesn’t argue. He is stood with a club in hand. She throws it over and he catches it left-handed. The other lefty means business.

“Agh Daniel come on the games up. There is nowhere to go” it dawns on O’ Par that of course it’s ridiculous to suspect a 70-year-old man of murder. A sweet old dancing grandad. Especially when face to face with a young violent angry man with a killer golf swing…literally a killer golf swing. He is holding a club from the bag strapped to the buggy. It’s one of Gabe’s clubs. She can’t see what he has selected but in his hands it’s a weapon to be wary of.

“There is always somewhere to go” Daniel James proclaims.

“I quite fancy paying Augusta” he adds.

“Agh Daniel the US are quite strict when it comes to visas… especially for murderers.” Gabe is totally lost. “What is going on” he asks…

“I am no murderer” Daniel James declares full of animosity.

“Well, that might have been the case…until you murdered four people.”

“Will somebody tell me what is going on…. Daniel” Gabe pleads.

“Gabe, dude. I love you. I did it to protect us. What we had. I just wanted to remove the footage. How dare they laugh at you. It was just jealousy.” Daniel James is turning and walking towards the buggy. He stops. "Well, that was the plan but that oaf. Flannery. He not only refused to hand his phone over, he then told me about the pictures of me. They had a secret meeting in the Members bar. They saw photos of me. They found out about my past somehow and they were going to let you know Gabe that I was trouble."

Gabe is about to say something, but he is lost for words. "And then he turned his back on me and told me to kiss his arse".

"But Daniel, I don't care about your past. I don't..."

"Stay here and you won't get hurt" he addresses both of them.

"There is no escaping" O' Par adds. "This is silly."

Daniel James throws O' Par's phone in the buggy. "See you around. Gabe, it's been a pleasure."

"Daniel. Where are you going."

"I am going on tour Gabe."

And with that Daniel James is thundering down the fairway at speed heading back to the clubhouse. Gabe's clubs are rattling around in the back. Jenny O' Par is running as fast and she can after the buggy. It's no use. She is not going to catch him. She stops and looks around. On the neighbouring fairway she sees a greenkeeper's truck.

She screams as she approaches. Clubhouse now …please. And a slightly bemused greenkeeper doesn't disappoint. After all, just the day before Alan had discovered a dead body in the 18th Greenside bunker. Gabe is struggling to keep up and is left behind.

Back at the tenth hole. Eagle has gone from thinking they might need to hand their badges in for letting a 70-year-old grandpa escape them to procuring as many buggies as he can. They set off in 5 buggies out on the course. Where's the fuck is O' Par. He is calling her but there is no answer.

The closer he gets to the clubhouse, Daniel James feels penned in. Sirens can be heard in the distance. There are police officers searching the woods down one side of the complex. Daniel James heads towards the Spa and Buggy shed on the opposite end of the complex and then when he sees a police officer wonder out of the pro shop, he spins the buggy around. He dumps it somewhere between the marquee and the bridge on the 18th. Behind him he can see O' Par has caught a lift and is on a truck trundling up the 18th.

Daniel James makes the fires escape on foot and heads up. He doesn't stop. Onwards and well upwards. He knows how to make it onto the top of the building. Many years ago, he would tee it up and hit balls from a makeshift tee off of the top of the roof out onto the course. Below him he can hear the police in pursuit. They are not going to catch him. He won't give the chance.

Back at the clubhouse after spotting O' Par racing in the opposite direction up the 18th in pursuit of Daniel James who had a decent head start Eagle was relieved to find O' Par safe and well. A few moments later Gabe joins them. DI Flog had picked him up. Eagle took a moment to gather his thoughts.

"Ok I want O' Par to go up with Gabe, since he is our best hope of getting through to Daniel. There are two officers waiting up there. He won't let them out. Says he is going to jump if they go any further." And then he adds "Be careful, any threat to Gabe or you leave immediately." He looked around, the top of the building looked out onto the lawn. A marquee filled the space. The other side of the building was a sheer drop which would drop you right outside reception. He stationed officers on all sides.

"I guess keep him talking. Try and get him down…until we have a better plan."

With Gabe in tow O' Par made it to the top of the stairs. Two officers stood by the door leading out to the rooftop. A couple of deep breaths. And she opened the door. “Don’t come any closer.” Daniel James shouts over.

“Daniel, it’s just Gabe and I.”

No response.

“We just want to make sure you are ok.”

“Why wouldn’t I be ok.” Daniel James laughs. O’ Par opens the door wide enough to see Daniel James is leaning, teetering over the edge at the back of the complex overlooking the lawn and the newly erected marquee to his right and the 18th Green on his left.

“We are going to come out”. Silence. “Is that Ok Daniel.”

“Not you. Only Gabe.” Daniel James is slowly thinking of a plan. Gabe appears and takes a couple of steps out onto the roof. He is certainly out of his comfort zone.

“That’s far enough” Daniel James asserts. “I tell you what Gabe for old times’ sake. One last reel.”

Gabe doesn’t like seeing Daniel like this. “Daniel come down. We can sort this out”.

“I wish Gabe. We are a little past that now buddy”.

“DCI O’ Par…” Daniel James calls out.

“I’m here” she replies.

“Gabe needs his clubs. And we need one of the practice mats from the pro shop”.

“Ok give me a minute. Daniel would this not be easier if we did this on ground level…. I know my legs would feel a lot better.”

“Nice try detective.” O’ Par gives the officer instructions to locate Gabe’s clubs from the buggy and return with them and a practice mat.

Eagle radios through and the other officer passes it over. “What’s going on Jenny.” He sounds stressed.

“Agh you know me just having the craic”.

“We don’t really want another body on our hands.”

“I think we are going to play some golf first.”

“What…can’t you just offer him a date if he comes down.”

“Stop would you. I am not sure he is my type after all.”

Outside on the roof Gabe and Daniel are talking. It’s as if nothing has happened. Perhaps O’ Par should take the opportunity to try and sneak out. An out of breath officer returns before she has made up her mind. He is carrying Gabe’s clubs and a little mat from the Pro Shop.

"I'm coming out" and she emerges. It's hot. The sun is shining. Blue sky. "What a view from up here."

"I know right" Daniel James is at home up here. "I used to come up here and hit a few balls when no one else was on the course.... that's far enough officer. Gabe can get them from there. We are going to sign off with one final reel. Well, I am going to sign off. This legend"... he nods at Gabe. "This legend has another 8 million followers in him."

Daniel James gives Gabe instructions to set up the mat. Jenny O' Par takes a few steps back towards the door as instructed by Daniel James. The target is the stream across the 18th fairway. He takes out his phone and plays around with it. "It won't be as good as the work phone Gabe but the view will make up for it. As pretty as you are detective you are not needed for this one".

Daniel James looks over the edge at those below. "Watch out below" Gabe tees up a ball. And Daniel James says a few words to the camera he tells everyone what a joy it is to work with Gabe and that Triple G has so much more to come (pause) watch him smash it out of the park" and over to Gabe who drives the ball into the sunshine down the 18th Fairway.

“Fore” Daniel James cries. He uploads the video and promotes it to live. “Nice One Gabe.”

“Right Daniel. Time to come down now.”

“I don’t think so Jenny” and unexpectedly and without hesitation Daniel James launches himself over the edge with a leap powered by his legs and arms in unison.

“Jaysus, what the”… she doesn’t finish.

“Daniel” Gabe calls out. Jenny O’ Par rushes to the edge expecting the worst. She can’t believe what he has just done.

Daniel James has surprised those down below not just the police officers who were on standby but the staff busying themselves decorating the marquee were equally surprised. Daniel James had launched himself off the roof onto the marquee crashing down so that it took his weight, momentarily threatening to catapult him back up before it semi collapsed under his weight, and then regaining its shape and structure allowing him to slide down safely to the ground. It was some leap of faith.

Daniel James hit the ground running and ran for the only place he knew he had the upper hand, the practice area. To get there the quickest way was to shoot across the range. Once clear he would be able to take a vehicle from the ground staff from the machine bay. He would be halfway across the course and on the farm track that led all the way to the village before they could figure out how to follow him. He had a good head start. No one below could quite believe what had happened. By the time Eagle sent his officers after him Daniel James had put nearly 50 yards between them. The range was within reach. He was going to escape.

Daniel James bounded onto the range and headed for the practice ground. He was extending his lead.

Jed was bored of waiting. In truth he was also still quite sore at learning that the weekend competition had been scrapped. Sure, he understood people had died, but also that shouldn't detract from his achievements on the course. Practice makes perfect. He had the bug. He headed to the range and was halfway through a basket of 100 balls. Boom. Another one out of the centre. Oh God he thought to himself tracing the ball. One of the staff was out there running…he was running straight into the trajectory of the ball…. "Fore" Jed's voice was a little hoarse, so he tried again this time full gusto. "FORE!" at the top of his voice.

Why was someone pelting it across the range. Two other runners appeared on the range but a good 100 yards behind.... Jed wasn't quite sure what was going on, but he had hit hard and true, he was after all in the ball striking form of his life And this one was right on target it bounced, thankfully falling short of the guy running, but it took a wicked bounce forward right and a then a ricochet off the target board saw it fly back into the direction of the runner hitting him full in the face dropping him on impact. Oh, shit thought Jed .... the two people running caught up with the injured party and more people started to swarm onto the range. What the heck is going on. Oh jeez. God No. There is no sign of life from the lump on the ground. Just my luck thought Jed. It's the bloody rozzers. A hole-in-one followed by killing someone on the range. How bloody inconsiderate.

"I did shout" he called out. "I did shout FORE."

Epilogue

The 19th Hole

"You know what they say about big hitters…the woods are full of them."

The woods that ran along the left-hand side of the tenth hole at Chorus Hills Golf and Country Club were indeed full of golf balls. They were also home to a bloody golf towel and packaging for a pack of Titleist ProV1s hidden in there by a murderer trying to cover his tracks.

The woods just to the edge of the 18th hole gave up Tom O Keefe's phone. Tom Noonan had indeed seen the last flash of light before the phone had gone to sleep. It turned out that O Keefe's phone revealed several pictures taken of photos hanging up in the members bar featuring Daniel James and a screenshot of a story about a young golfer turning violent during a county match.

Daniel James' touchscreen gloves featuring Triple G's distinctive logo were found stowed away in the buggy he had borrowed for his early morning joyride. The fabric matched the fibres found on the golf balls retrieved from the deceased. Not that there was any doubt.

Green liked joining up all the dots. Shame about those Pro V1s.

A visibly shaken Gabe joined the other members of the Society in the 19th for a stiff drink in the aftermath of the chase. Daniel James has been arrested but was heading straight to the hospital after a nasty injury to the side of his head. Jed was relieved that he hadn't killed anyone though there were some concerns about Daniel James eyesight. He had taken a hefty blow in his right eye socket. Jed had received a few pats on the back for his efforts on the Range. Not many people can claim to have taken down a multiple murderer. News spread fast. Triple G's latest reel had been watched over 1.5 million times in little over an hour. The agency was having trouble debating the ethics of the piece versus the number of hits.

Gabe would of course be sorry to not have Daniel around anymore but he, and especially Triple G, couldn't condone murder. Or any kind of violence. After all Daniel had gone on to kill 4 people that Gabe had known for at least twenty years. Nevertheless, if he was honest Gabe would miss Daniel more than his fallen comrades. That particular fourball at any rate.

Eagle and O' Par joined the Society members in the 19th. No one was happier to see them than Tom Noonan. There were all manner of different groups congregating in the bar. Perhaps the best part of Whackfuck after all. Eagle was looking forward to a cold pint. It wasn't quite knocking off time. Jed was still whining about not winning the weekend competition and after saying their goodbyes the two officers crept off to a quiet corner. It had been quite a shock and a testament to the group that they were still trying to share laughs, memories and planning for their next away weekend after all that had happened. Eagle just hoped when that time came it would be in a different County.

O' Par sat opposite Eagle and the two of them looked out of the window out onto the 18th green and the bridge over the moat. And the bunker. Michael Flannery's bunker. I don't think anyone else will be calling it that. It was unlikely that a plaque would be erected.

"Well at least there is nothing spoiling the view today. The Commissioner will be pleased ahead of his round tomorrow". It had been a long day. "Shall we partake in the 19th."

"Sure, why not" O' Par answered her boss.

The original Augusta was intended to have a 19th hole, giving losing golfers a chance to win their money back on a quick round of double-or-nothing. It was indefinitely tabled because the hole would ruin the flow of the golf course. The two colleagues sat with two cold beers in front of them.

"Well, you owe me dinner Detective Chief Superintendent Nik Eagle."

"Double or nothing". Eagle replied.

"Ok if you can get within 100,000 dinner is on me." O' Par runs her fingers through her hair.

"100,000 of what" Eagle can tell he is being set up.

"How many views on Triple G's latest reel. Daniel James' last video edit."

He may as well admit defeat. "Ok I will go for a nice round 1 million."

"Hey that's not bad for you but you are half a mill out" looking pleased with herself O' Par added "That's two dinners."

Eagle smiled "I can offer you a Chinese at mine. I promised Fin I would be back on time tonight. I can't risk another protest poo."

"Wait why are you doing a protest poo" O Par is laughing at her own joke. "Ok you are on. But I am not cleaning up dog poo and don't for a second think that you are getting away with taking me out out you tight arse. I fancy hitting a few balls and then dinner at a nice golf club", she laughed again… "now that you know so much about golf."

"Temporary insanity practiced on a cow pasture."

"Agh the fresh air would do you good."

"Maybe I will see if Ian Woosnam is free."

"That's it… the sum of your total knowledge of golfers."

"I could ask that Fuzzy guy, or Lefty, or the Walrus."

"Jaysus how about someone from this century."

"OK OK that Rory Macintosh or how about Tiger Woods."

"Oh, Wow am I meant to be impressed that you have heard of him."

A missed call pops up from the Commissioner. "Good job reception here is bad."

"Don't I know it". A text message pops up and Eagle reads it aloud. 'Well done. Good job'.

"Jaysus.. O' Par contemplates "I guess winning takes care of everything… even with that Amadan." Eagle nods about to add his own assessment but he knows better than to try and get the last word "That's a Tiger Wood's quote…. well except the Amadan bit. I added that for you."

Glossary

Amadan – Idiot (see also Eejit) from Middle Irish *ammatán ("fool, simpleton").

Bogey – A score of one stroke over par at a hole. "Well at least it wasn't a double bogey".

Cockwomble - A person, usually male, who is prone to making outrageously stupid statements and-or inappropriate behaviour while having a very high opinion of their own wisdom and importance.

Cop on - Cop on' is a general catch-all term for having some common sense or intelligence in any situation. If you're behaving foolishly, you'll be told to 'cop on'.

Dryshite – A person who is boring and no fun.

Eagle – A score two strokes under Par for the hole. For most of us golfers rarer than hen's teeth.

Eejit – A stupid person; an idiot (see also Amadan) "don't stand there like a gormless eejit!"

Feck - A less serious alternative to the expletive "fuck" to express disbelief, surprise, pain, anger, or contempt. When said in an Irish accent it's barely even an expletive.

Fuzzy Zoeller - Frank Urban "Fuzzy" Zoeller Jr is an American professional golfer who has won ten PGA Tour events including two Major championships. He is one of only 3 golfers to win the Masters tournament at his first attempt playing the event.

Gobshite – A person who is stupid or says silly things, a numpty.

Gombeen – Shady small-time wheeler-dealer

GUR – Ground Under Repair.

Ian Woosnam - Ian Harold Woosnam OBE, is a Welsh professional golfer and golf course designer. Nicknamed 'Woosie', Woosnam won the US Masters tournament in 1991.

James Joyce- James Joyce was an Irish novelist praised for his intellect and wit. However, his work is lost on many readers who find it difficult to understand and follow. In golfing terms it references putting lines that are near impossible to judge or which cannot be read.

Lefty - Phil Mickelson, a right-handed 6-time Major Championships winner who plays golf left-handed and is known as Lefty.

Pro V1s – An expensive golf ball guaranteed to take numerous shots off your game. Nobody likes to lose a Pro V1, but equally finding one on the course is better than finding a rare white truffle, especially as you can't hit your provisional using a rare white truffle.

Shitehawk – A purveyor of shite.

SIO – Senior Investigating Officer.

The Walrus – Craig Robert Stadler is an American professional golfer who has won numerous tournaments at both the PGA Tour and Champions Tour level, including one Major championship, the 1982 Masters Tournament and was known by the nickname 'The Walrus', on account of his portly build and ample moustache.

Whackfuck – Golf.

"Golf can best be defined as an endless series of tragedies obscured by the occasional miracle."

"Of all the hazards, fear is the worst."

ISBN: 978-1-66640-524-8

Printed in Great Britain
by Amazon

29799893R00116